FREDERIC RAPHAEL was born in
to England as a boy. He was
School and St John's College, Cambridge. His fiction
includes *The Earlsdon Way, The Limits of Love, Lindmann, Like Men Betrayed, Heaven and Earth, A Double
Life, Old Scores* and *Coast to Coast* and several collections
of short stories. He is also well known for his screen-
writing for film and television including *Darling, Far
from the Madding Crowd, Two for the Road, Rogue Male*
and *Eyes Wide Shut*. His memoir of the collaboration
with director Stanley Kubrick on the screenplay of *Eyes
Wide Shut* was published in 1999 as *Eyes Wide Open*. His
novel *The Glittering Prizes*, which tells the stories of a
group of Cambridge undergraduates in post-war Britain,
was made into a BBC television series in 1976 and won a
Royal Television Society Award (Writer of the Year). Its
sequels, *Fame and Fortune* and *Final Demands*, were
adapted for radio.

He has also written history books, including *Some
Talk of Alexander*, an overview of the Ancient Greece,
and *A Jew Among Romans: The Life and Legacy of Flavius
Josephus*, together with a number of translations from
the classics. Author of many essays and articles, Raphael
is a frequent reviewer in the *Literary Review*, the *Times
Literary Supplement*, the *Wall Street Journal* and elsewhere. He has written biographies of Byron and Somerset
Maugham, and his autobiographical work includes six
volumes in the *Personal Terms* series and the memoir *A
Spoilt Boy*, which covers the first eighteen years of his
life. The second volume of his autobiography, *Going Up*,
is being published in 2015.

Fiction by the same author

Novels
Obbligato
The Earlsdon Way
The Limits of Love
A Wild Surmise
The Graduate Wife
The Trouble with England
Lindmann
Darling
Orchestra and Beginners
Like Men Betrayed
Who Were You With Last Night?
April, June and November
Richard's Things
California Time
The Glittering Prizes
Heaven and Earth
After the War (also adapted for television)
The Hidden I
A Double Life
Old Scores
Coast to Coast
Fame and Fortune
Final Demands

Short stories
Sleeps Six
Oxbridge Blues (also published as scripts of TV plays)
Think of England
The Latin Lover
All His Sons

PRIVATE VIEWS

FREDERIC RAPHAEL

PETER OWEN
London and Chicago

PETER OWEN PUBLISHERS
81 Ridge Road, London N8 9NP

Peter Owen books are distributed in the USA and Canada by
Independent Publishers Group/Trafalgar Square
814 North Franklin Street, Chicago, IL 60610, USA

First published in Great Britain 2015 by
Peter Owen Publishers

© Volatic Ltd 2015

PAPERBACK ISBN 978-0-7206-1853-2
EPUB ISBN 978-0-7206-1852-5
MOBIPOCKET ISBN 978-0-7206-1854-9
PDF ISBN 978-0-7206-1855-6

A catalogue record for this book is available
from the British Library

Typeset by Octavo Smith Publishing Services
www.octavosmith.com

Printed and bound in the UK by
CPI Group (UK) Ltd, Croydon, CR0 4YY

'L'amant, c'est celui qui attend.'
– Roland Barthes

For Sarah

1

Soon after two-thirty on a Saturday afternoon in early summer, two boys from a nearby public school, out on their bicycles, were overtaken by a new red Triumph Herald as it drove through Shackleford. A young couple sat in the front seats, the black canvas roof folded behind them. The Herald went on along the Hurtmore road towards the junction with the A3. The boys heard the aggravated howl of a lorry's horn, a glassy metallic crash and then loud silence. They stood on their pedals to accelerate to the scene. A heavy lorry had tilted but not fallen over. The front of the car was compressed under the elevated cab.

The younger, more handsome boy dropped his 'grid' – his school's slang for bicycle – in the ditch and ran, as if he would be faster on foot, up the hundred yards back along the Hurtmore road, to a thickly thatched tea-room. He pulled down the metal handle of the bell-pull sleeved against the brickwork and, at the same time, knuckled the studded oak door. He stood on one leg and then the other to take off his bicycle-clips. After some seconds, a woman in a floral cotton wrapper and rayon stockings, roused from rest, unlocked the door.

'There'd better be a good reason, that's all.'

The panting boy told her that there had been a road accident and then pointed towards the A3. They needed to call the police and an ambulance. The woman scowled at such an unarguable excuse. The boy stood there in his brown herringbone tweed suit, bicycle clips in his left hand, while she went inside. Saturday afternoon, the girl at the local exchange was slow to answer. It gave time for the woman to glare at the boy.

The police and ambulance crew had to summon lifting gear before they could right the lorry, which was loaded with twin-tub washing machines, and ease the bodies from the wreckage.

'Both dead?'

'Both dead.'

By the side of the road, the lorry-driver was shaking his head. He told the police sergeant that the Triumph had driven straight out across the STOP line; he had had no time to avoid it. He didn't know what his guv'nor was going to say about all this. Was there a telephone box near by? He'd hurt his knee, but he was OK to walk to anywhere close. 'Came straight out,' he said. 'Didn't give me no chance whatsoever.' The silent witnesses – short scorch marks on the macadam immediately before the point of collision – confirmed his account.

After the bodies had been loaded into the ambulance, the driver returned and resumed shaking his head. The lorry's windscreen was cracked, diagonally, from top right to bottom left, but the rig seemed safe to drive. The driver left his details with the police and was allowed to continue on his way. Half an hour later a Godalming garage-man hoisted the flattened front end of the Triumph off the road and hauled the wreck away. The two youngest policemen were left to sweep nuggets of red and white broken glass off the tarmac. 'That's it then, basically.'

Back at the police station, an inspector telephoned the mother of the dead woman to inform her that her daughter and son-in-law were 'unfortunately dead'.

She said, 'What about Karen? Is she all right?'

'Karen?'

'Their little girl. They were all three coming to see us.'

'We didn't see any little girl.'

'Five years old. I know she was with them.'

The young policemen were sent back to the Hurtmore road. There was a long, thick cuff of hedge on each side of the junction with the trunk road. They scouted along both roads before they spotted the little girl. Her legs were folded in the dry ditch on the far side of the hedge; her head and shoulders nestled among the foliage. The impact must have thrown her across the road and into the soft cover. She had her two fists under her chin. Unblinking eyes were staring at where the two roads met.

'Hullo. We're policemen. And you have to be Karen. We've come to take care of you. Are you hurt?'

Chin still lodged on her fists, she shook her head to the smallest possible degree.

'Can you . . . come out of there and . . . we'll . . . we'll look after you?'

'I want to stay here.'

'You'd be better with your granny.'

'I want to stay here.'

'She wants to . . . wants to see you and . . . look after you.'

'Granny who?'

The younger policeman said, 'Your mum's mum.'

'I want to stay here.'

'No, you don't, not really.'

'I shouldn't've talked to Daddy, should I?'

'It wasn't your fault, Karen.'

'I heard you say.'

'No one said that.'

'"Both dead," you said.'

'Let's get you out of there. Careful of the . . . '

'Ninety-six.'

'Ninety-six what, Karen?'

'Cars, in both directions, since it happened. That's ninety-seven.'

2

She was painting a naked man with many golden curls. He sat on a reversed wooden kitchen chair, legs apart, thick feet flat on the floor. She used a fine brush to catch the highlight on the purple bud of the penis which was pressing the whitish foreskin slightly open. The studio was a large first-floor room in Redcliffe Gardens. Traffic went by, stopped, went on by.

She said, 'Don't move. I haven't done.'

'I wasn't,' the man said. 'Not on purpose.'

'Also don't talk, Mal. It changes your face.'

'I didn't know you were painting it.'

'The face changes, everything changes.'

'It's your fault. If anything moved.'

She cleaned her brush on a rag and looked at her work. 'Can you come Wednesday afternoon?'

'I can do an hour; have to be away by five.'

'Wednesday afternoon then.'

'You know what you are. I know: you know.'

She said, 'I don't mind painting you with an erection; but if you have one you'll have to . . .'

'Keep it up?'

'Once you . . .'

'Then I'll have to . . . try and . . . not think about you.'

'Up to you,' she said.

3

Charlie Marsden said, 'Listen, Marco, if we're going, time we were.'

'Are we walking?'

'Do us good, unfortunately.'

'We'll grab a cab then. Do I need a scrape?'

'Onslow Gardens? You look adequately scraped already. Verging on natty. I'd gladly chuck, but I promised Milly we'd be on time.'

They shared top-floor rooms at 15 Beaufort Street. Steele was slim and dark. Charlie had accused him, once or twice, of resembling an Edwardian jockey gone to seed: he had the longish, straight and narrow nose, keen eyes, black hair and that way of standing with both fists in front of his thighs, as if with an invisible whip between them. His face had a luminous whiteness, lips deep purple and definite, mole on the left cheek. Sporting the air of a dandy who had chosen his own physical features, he wore a single-breasted charcoal Douggie Hayward suit: narrow lapels, slim legs (no turn-ups), elongated jacket with one vent, four grey bone buttons down the front.

Marcus did go and have a scrape all the same. Charlie was damned if Theo's thrash warranted changing from Chelsea boots, fawn cavalry twill trousers, check shirt, tally-ho silk square and double-breasted black jacket, black buttons. He put on a check Raglan coat and a flat cap on top of his bouncy light-brown hair. Charlie's careless outdoor appearance contrasted, to one or the other's advantage, with Marcus's curt charcoal-grey overcoat with red lining and velvet facings.

Having been there more than a few times, they took the insider's way to Ferdy Plant's place: through Onslow Gardens and then up a pierced cast-iron ladder to a first-floor walkway. A short stroll took them towards the back entrance of the domed reception room where the party was already in vocal progress.

'The sweet sound of rhubarb,' Charlie said, 'at all but full volume. What's that music wafting in from somewhere? I recognize it, but I can't say what it is. Your department that, never mine. Knowing those things.'

'Mozart's *Jupiter*,' Marcus said. 'Symphony 41 in C major. T.E.'s favourite number when he was at Clouds Hill. K551.'

'For Christ's sake, never get in trouble with the police, Marco. You'll only volunteer more information than you're asked for and get yourself caught low down at second slip.'

On the far side of the private gardens two fair young men were drinking yellow wine in green-stemmed glasses. The one in a white towelling robe was stretched on a black metal *chaise longue*, bare feet up on the terrace railing; the other was leaning against a French door in a white aertex shirt, tennis shorts and a long-sleeved cable-stitched Old Carthusian cricket-club sweater, pale pink stripes in the regulation places. The 'hasher' had vertical slits on each side; the wearer could cover his bum and put his hands in his pockets at the same time.

A slim young woman, in a yellow-and-green flowered silk dress with a long skirt, was seated on the stone parapet, back to the gardens. One haunch overlapped the stonework by the first young man's clean feet. She was stroking the nearer one, like a kitten. The young man in the O.C. hasher extracted his right hand from his pocket and played Marcus a set of scales in the air. Marcus gave a shrug and a lift of the jaw. 'Reminds me of "Cuddles" Browning that one.'

Something the slim woman saw in the tennis player's eye impelled her to turn to have a look. A low ray of April sunlight glinted on a small silver spoon hanging on a fine chain around her neck. She inspected Marcus, closed one nostril with a long finger and drew breath, with a necessary wink. The man in the ribbed sweater took a step forward and kissed the woman on the shoulder, at length, eyes on Marcus.

'*Tutti assieme* possibilities, it looks to me,' Charlie said. 'Far as you're concerned. Three to tango time.'

A few yards short of the swell of the dome, a trio of ribbed terracotta amphorae were crowned with bushy camellia plants; buds striated with white veins, furled petals pressing to burst out. Weathered casts of a piping Silenus and a disarmed nymph stood sentinel at the top of a metal ladder down to a discreet door into the domed room. Marcus thumbed the nymph's right nipple *en passant*. 'Were you breast-fed at all, Carlos?'

'Not recently.'

'I went with a milky lady on one occasion. Had to miss my innings. Funny affair, bed!'

'Yes,' Charlie Marsden said. 'I'd just as soon break-fast myself.'

The tight door opened into the back of the domed room. Slim, fluted white pillars supported the points at which six spokes, spreading down from the hexa-gonal lantern at the summit of the dome, met the steel hoop inscribed within the square room. The centre of attention among the twenty or so people already at the party was a stretched, gaunt, chalky-faced man in a crushed-raspberry corduroy suit and bullfighter's frilled shirt and stringy tie. He held a long black Dun-hill cigarette holder, silver-banded, between unusual fingers.

'Oh Christ,' Charlie said. 'B-Benny Bligh in f-full f-flow and f-fuller fig! Shall we adjourn? *Sine die* suits me.'

'*Noblesse oblige*, Charles.'

'Yes; I do wish it wouldn't keep doing that.'

The party was to celebrate the publication of Ferdy Plant's new North Oxford thriller, *Whodunnit?* Half-open copies were on stiff parade, upright in yellow jackets, at the back of a sheeted trestle table. Glasses, bottles and colourful cold canapés waited for custom. Ferdy's culinary brother Theo, in a vertically striped black-and-yellow waistcoat, a chafing dish of hot snacks on either hand, was standing in for hired help.

'Author! Author!'

Ferdy, in plum velvet smoking jacket and black trousers, came to them. 'If it ain't the Hon Charles

Marsden! And . . . who's your pushy friend again?'

Marcus said, 'Careful, Ferdinand, how far you go, in which direction and up to what point. Otherwise feel free. What do you call these prune jobs of yours with bacon wrapped round them?'

'Fred mostly, don't I? Charlie? Care for anything?'

'God, yes!' Charlie was looking across the room at a dark-haired woman wearing a purple woollen dress, cinched with a wide black leather belt. She was crouching down, with elastic ease, one shining knee a touch in advance of the other, one stiletto heel cocked in the air, while she admired a makeshift book of crayoned drawings, composed of sheets of white paper folded in half. The pages were being turned for her approval by Ferdy's seven-year-old, Francesca.

'In my pri-pri-private view,' Benedict Bligh was being heard to say, 'sexual passion is something – unlike p-pretty p-pollytics – we should never take with undue seriousness. The erotic should, I c-consider, always be subsumed under the ludic.'

'Spelt l–e–w–d, in your case, Benedict, presumably.'

'Emma must try harder, her last report said, and that, g-goodness knows, Emma is certainly doing!'

'Must you always be beastly to people?'

'Only what one chooses to do is what one has to do.'

'Remind me why that's ever so wise and witty.'

'I shall remind you, should you elect to take that course, my p-pretty one, with corrective severity; if necessary in F-French.'

'I expected the Poms to talk a lot of balls,' Doris

Vreeland said, 'but why do some of them have to do it all the time?'

'Because that's what editors pay them for; in your case, digger Doris, so rumour promises, by the bush-hole.'

The woman in the purple dress closed the book of drawings but remained on a level with its author. Compressed in an elegant, seamless S, she was talking to little Francesca, with eloquent fingers, about her 'picture story'. At length she straightened, easily, just as Charlie was taking a step in her direction. Benedict Bligh was watching, and talking, while she walked, high on those heels, across the room. She went past him and then in front of Charlie Marsden to the far side of the cupola where double doors gave access to Ferdy's drawing-room.

The man who stepped into the room as she approached was of no more than medium height but thick in the chest and shoulders. His wide-lapelled, double-breasted, unduly blue suit had pinstripes too white and too wide for Charlie's taste. His thick tie carried discordant scrawls of colour. The woman in purple went up to him and took his arm. No, he would not come into the room. No, he did not want a drink.

Charlie was eating a prune snack – '*Négresses en chemise*, possibly, are they called, or should be?' – as the rare-looking woman continued to talk to the unlikely man. It seemed that she left spaces for him to answer without expecting him to do so. No word of what she was saying quite reached Charlie's ears, but her intonation was coaxing. Although she was taller, the man seemed to stand over her. Was she convent-educated, possibly? The man was scanning the company without interest.

Charlie said, 'Tell me something, cook: who's that menacing personage who's not quite with us and what's a goddess doing talking to him?'

Theo considered the matter. 'Her charioteer might he be?'

Benedict Bligh was saying, 'Greater love hath no man than this, that he l-lay down his w-w-wife for his friend. As D-Doris here will tell you and anyone else she happens to straddle.'

'Know something, Emma?' Doris Vreeland said. 'Until I came across Benedict I'd never met a banana that could stammer.'

'The last time you came across anybody, Doris,' Benedict said, 'it was – if reports be true – a fellow ostrich in return for a two-day-old sarnie in the Earls Court Road; *orf.*'

'And he expects people to like him!' Emma Ringrose said.

'*Lick* him, dear, is what it says on my hymn sheet.'

'Charlie Marsden, can it be?'

'Tamsin Fairfax, can it not? Whose bandbox have you just stepped out of? You've decided to stand up and be Quanted, is my guess.'

'If I'd known B. Bligh esquire was going to be here I'm not sure that I should have come at all.'

'You speak for us all. How's Master Humphrey?'

'Still watching the same old bloody clock.'

'Hence not among us this evening?'

'If he ever leaves the office, even for a second, it's not for any reason he chooses to tell me about.'

'I can imagine.'

The woman in purple had been to the buffet. She was carrying a flute of Louis Roederer to where the solid pinstriped man was still standing against the doorpost. He made no move to concede space as a pretty, hot girl, fawn fun-fur round her shoulders, hurried into the room. The only effect of her advent was, it seemed, to make him draw back his cuff and look at his big watch. The woman in purple did not contradict him, but she did sip some of the champagne which he had ignored.

The pretty girl's large escort followed her, slowly, into the white room, also looking hot. His uneven duffel coat had black stains on it. He held up oil-smudged hands in explanatory surrender.

Charlie said, 'Hullo, sis. What happened to six-thirty at the latest?'

'We'd have been here,' Camilla said, 'with oceans of it to spare, but Perry had a puncture.'

'He doesn't seem to have gone down all that much. How are you, Peregrine, apart from the nail in your tread?'

'In urgent need of a corner. What's the geography?'

Theo indicated to go through the double doors and sharp right.

Charlie said, 'Sister, tell me something of rather more than the first importance. Who is that?'

'Katya Lowell, do you mean?'

'Katya Lowell, who is . . .'

'Very famous actually.'

'Since when and for what?'

'Since my trumpet sounded about her last show in *Town* magazine. Her work is truly remarkable. The Lady Fatso wrote her up in the *ST* and pinched several of my lines. I made quite a stink.'

'The smells I miss!'

'You make rather a point of it, I sometimes think. Wherever have you been? Anywhere interesting?'

'Connemara, haven't I?'

'Oh, 'course! How did you find our noble papa?'

'By the luminosity of his nose, how else?'

'And how is the Dong, what there is of him?'

'Still pouring it out and putting it away.'

'I hope you gave him my.'

'And he duly sent you his. I hope it was his.'

'And who's that she's with, do you know at all, the painter lady?'

'Looks suspiciously like a bee's-knees-man to me.'

Marcus put a finger on Camilla's pink woolly shoulder. 'Still speaking kiddish, you two, do I gather?'

Camilla said, 'And why should we not, dear Marcus, dear Marcus, why should we not? Why grow up before one has to?'

Marcus said, 'That pretty Tamsin does know about Master Humphrey's cock as well, I take it, as the irregular hours it strikes?'

'Presumably.'

'She's being very plucky, in that case. Taking it in good part, as they say. Is she rogering jollily at all, do we know?'

'Not that I've . . .'

'Time she did then,' Marcus said.

'I think she blames herself,' Camilla said.

'Very little charge to be gained from that. Opening for a likely lad, conceivably.'

'You never know. What's become of Charlesworth suddenly?'

4

Charlie had walked through the double doors into the unlit elderly drawing-room of Ferdy's shadowy house. He unlatched the french windows and stepped out on to the small square terrace over the front door and its three wide, thick-lipped steps to the pavement. Katya Lowell was standing a few yards short of a lustrous blue Bristol with K licence plates. The pinstriped man was unlocking the door. Katya, standing taller in a Cossack hat, was looking in Charlie's direction but never at him, a dark-brown, fur-trimmed coat slung around her shoulders; the long fingers of her right hand clasped its suede wings together at the waist.

There was a beep on the Bristol's horn. The pinstriped man was already at the wheel. Katya regathered her coat but did not shift her stance. Charlie leaned with both hands on the wide balustrade of the narrow terrace. The Bristol's horn sounded again, louder and longer. Katya looked amused, never entertained. Charlie smiled downwards, not at her, enjoying the closet play.

After a minute, she consented to get into the car. The Bristol backed a yard and then, trailing a noisy billow of exhaust, pulled out of the parking space and surged down the street towards the Fulham Road. A few seconds later a motorbike started up, somewhere to the left, and took the same course. The rider and the person riding pillion were in chromium-studded black leather.

As they came level with Charlie, the pillion rider raised two accurate fingers and made to pick him off.

When Charlie had found his way back to the domed room, Doris Vreeland was saying, 'Tell me, something, Benedict: how in heck do you get all those ladies to let you do the things you claim you do to them?'

'I make no claims whatever. Au c-contraire, I always g-guarantee discretion not to say anonymity. The claims, like the pleasure, are all theirs. Collusion is the key to the closet. That is part of the many things you will never understand, d-digger D-Doris.'

Tamsin Fairfax was a few feet away, not necessarily listening.

'I understand some of them may need the action,' Doris Vreeland said, 'but the baroness von Thingystein, for example, why would she deliver herself to be rouged by you?'

'The sex doesn't like to feel it's missing things,' Benedict said.

'But what do you say to persuade them to the . . . sticking point?'

'That's precisely what not a few of them are t-tempted to elicit. What better at the head of the garden path than a monkey-puzzle tree? "Tell me more" is then a prayer which I can but honour. I first arouse their . . . interest. In a third-partying, speculative, aesthetic sense.'

'And what does that take? One finger or two?'

Benedict said, 'You have the rasping subtlety, D-Doris d-darling, of a ventilating donkey. To someone of greater wit, I might suggest that there is nothing so shiversome and alluring as an imminent point of no return.'

Tamsin said, 'He does so make one want to be somewhere else doing something entirely different, does Master B.'

'I do the sex the honour of indulging their c-curiosity, which, you will almost certainly not remember, has an antique affinity with f-f-felicity.'

'Felicity who would that be?'

'Oh dear, oh d-d-definitely d-dear,' Benedict Bligh said.

Marcus had one hand, at arm's length, on a pillar, one boot crooked over the instep of the other. 'So, you and Perry've been partying and things, do I hear?'

'Partying, yes,' Camilla said, 'things, no. I love Perry with all my heart and soul, but it doesn't go an inch further than that.'

Marcus smiled and stood straight and pressed the flat of his right hand courteously between Camilla's thighs. She turned for a cigarette from the box at the end of the trestle table.

Doris was saying, 'And can you tell they're curious by just looking at them?'

Benedict said, 'By how they look at me.'

Tamsin leaned close for a light from Camilla's match. 'And then?'

'What they c-cannot at f-first imagine wanting anyone to do to them, they later come to . . . see me about. If we prove to be in happy c-conspiracy, I accept the c-commission, on my own strict terms, which is what, in their secret heats, they imagined. There's never any hurry. I like to talk and I like to have them talk. The menu should always precede the meal by a . . . s-salivatory quotient of expectant time. They are at liberty to mock and to say, at length, how mistaken I am about women. They go on, very often, until they need to be c-c-corrected. If they are p-piqued by that prospect, so be it. But they have to earn their stripes. Champagne can then be followed by the real thing.'

'Are you all right, Tamsin?'

'Right as Rhine, dear Charles. Why?'

'Katya Lowell. Tell me all.'

'She paints. Is all I know.'

'She also walks in beauty. What're they like, her paintings?'

'Unlike other people's. Might "cryptic" be the right word?'

'If you chose it, how should it not be?'

5

14. *The Rose at Its Peak Has Peaked*. The interior of a low-
ceilinged 1930s flat with off-white, stippled wallpaper;
a Crittall window in the background, a small harbour
and quay visible through the glass. Off-centre, to the
left, a slim naked woman, seen *de dos*, in a boudoir
chair: padded seat, bow-legs with claw feet over
castered balls. She is holding her deep-auburn hair
in both hands, up from her neck. The flesh of her
back is white; her buttocks and what can be seen of
her pursed sex are pink. On the table beside her is a
vase of white tulips. Some petals appear to have fallen
on to the surface of the table. They are blood red. 42
x 28. Acrylic on paper.

6

The top-floor flat at 15 Beaufort Street had the bachelor-
dom of an Oxford set. The furniture was old, little of it
antique. Marcus and Charlie had been obliged to buy
the sorry sofa and prolapsed armchairs from the
previous tenant. As the place was rent-controlled at the
time of purchase, they had had no choice if they
wanted to acquire the lease. Since then, Marcus had
picked up a few more comely pieces here and there. The
carved walnut *bergère* chair with the wickerwork seat
and sides was a thank-you from a client for how Marcus
had parlayed an unlikely lot well beyond its reserve.
The Cecil Aldin prints, George du Maurier cartoons and
variously framed Piranesi etchings had been lodged
with Charlie after his papa abandoned the family place
in Wiltshire and removed himself to untaxed Ireland.
As if to take the curse off their authenticity, the prints
were asymmetrically arranged and did not all hang
straight.

Charlie ate breakfast in pyjamas, crimson dressing-
gown and black house-slippers. By the time he had
carried his grandmother's tray, with its fruity silver
handles, to the drop-leaf table overlooking Beaufort
Street Marcus was already in his auctioneer's battle-
dress: slim grey suit, dark-blue shirt with stiff white
collar, knitted blue-black silk tie, haematite cufflinks.
He removed the Mitcheldene & Cleverley catalogue

from the burgundy-coloured table to his lap and slapped shut Edward Joy's Antique English Furniture. He had been verifying one or two items destined to fall under his hammer.

'So,' Charlie said, 'what brand of dead horse might you be flogging this morning, Master M?'

'Pride of place goes to a set of Sheraton dining-room chairs in mint condition. Among other antique items of recent manufacture. Does it matter?'

'List me what does,' Charlie said.

'Even most of what's guaranteed to be right is, like Theseus' ship, after a time more patch than original. But then who isn't?'

'You're way over my head, Marcus. Your intention, I presume.'

'You've guessed it.' Marcus looked at his flat watch and said, 'Charlie, before I go . . .'

'Say it,' Charlie said.

'Sharing this place with you . . .'

'Hasn't been one of the rare joys of your life, has it?'

'One of the rare instances of friction-free pleasure, shall we say?'

'And leave it at that? Or leave me, do I gather? Some sort of a Pole, is she, do I hear? Also perch, I suspect you're about to tell me, the rod being yours.'

'You, too, can be very elaborate when roused, can you not? All we have left from being educated in an obsolete school. I'd've said something sooner, but I assumed that you'd sooner hear an ugly rumour or two first. Dry the starting tear, I should. It'll suit you very nicely to have the place to yourself. You and Camilla are still coming to Potts this weekend, aren't you?'

'Had you heard differently?'

'Only you'll then get a chance to meet Anya.' Marcus replaced Joy's authoritative book of words on a long shelf adjacent to Charlie as he ate his Grape-Nuts, jaw going left to right and back again. Nanny Chisholm had used to call it 'milling like God'. Marcus looked at his nice flat watch and stood up. 'Funnily enough, Anya and my mama get on like a house on fire.'

'Why do houses on fire get on,' Charlie said, 'do you know at all? And, while you're at it, why do brass rags part? Not going to marry her or anything, are you?'

'Anything, certainly. Already have,' Marcus said, from where he was putting his coat on. 'Very continental she is, I'm rejoiced to say. No try she won't convert, no holes barred.' He went out and slammed the front door, only because he had to; otherwise it clicked and stayed ajar. One end of the shelf on which he had replaced the heavy volume sprang from the wall and shot its freight of books on to the parquet. Charlie finished his breakfast, scanned Fred Kirby's city column in the *Daily Crusader* and went to get ready to go to work at Norton, Wilment of 3 London Wall. That nice Mrs Thing would pick up the books when she came in later.

7

Tamsin Fairfax was a few deliberate minutes late for her meeting with Benedict Bligh in the palm court of the Waldorf Hotel. He had made himself lengthily at home on a settee and was reading the *New York Review of Books* for which he had composed 5,000 words on the uses of brevity in the drama, from Bérénice's 'Adieu' via Sartre's 'Donc, recommençons' to contemporary instances of 'sustained brevity and poignant pointlessness'. Even when Benedict held a newspaper he did so in a singular attitude.

'Unpredictable traffic!' Tamsin said.

'We are indeed,' Benedict said. 'Oh, I ordered china tea and a bourgeois selection of sandwiches. In a place like this one must strive to be unremarked.'

'Take your feet off the table then, I should, so he can put it down.'

'You be m-mother, seeing as . . . this was your idea.'

'I do hope you understand that the main, if not sole, reason I'm here is that I've been commissioned by Trevor to do this piece about you.'

'And it's of the essence that you depict me in a frowsty light, is that it?'

'When did you embark on your career of being caustic? Before or after you discovered you were an aristocratic by-blow?'

'Startling as we mean to go on, and on, is that the

plan, Mistress T? Here's the stock answer: if a man can't be sure of anything else, he can at least choose his style. Some touch wood, others touch bottom. You're not putting m-milk in it, and first, are you?'

'Do you think less of me?'

'How would I d-do that? And why would you want me to? Shall we analyse that? Your place or mine? Not here, dear, not here.'

'Seriously, Benedict . . .'

'Seriously is extra. And much less fun, possibly. What?'

'You obviously like people to know. The things you do with ladies. Or to them.'

'Some kiss, some tell. Score card, card of the match! Their decision, never mine.'

'Might it be that a lurid reputation is more important to you than what it's for?'

'Which is what?'

'*Aspro pato*, the Greeks call it, don't they?'

'Did you look that up in the hope of confounding me?'

'No need. Humph was second sec and bottle-washer in Athens for two years. Means "bottoms up", roughly. They did a lot of it in those days. And still do, I don't doubt.'

'Can be a living.'

'I would like to know the connection . . .'

'The g-great connection, Henry James called f-fucking. But only because he never d-did it, I suspect.'

'. . . Between being a critic and being a . . .'

'Find a nice word and it might have been worth c-coming.'

'How about a "wanton"?'

'Nobbad! A Chinese dish; quite appetising, I'm told. The essence, my dear Tamsin, of what I am out and about, *qua evangelista*, is the extirpation of muddle-class shame. Humbug goes back a long way and trails a blushing and reticent retinue in its striped wake. The critical moment – is that your "aha" look? – came in the Garden of Eden, when Adam looked to God to . . . oh, chasten Eve after her passade with the snake. At that point the female had trumped the male. Yet she never dared to assert as much. Did her nerve fail her, or might it possibly be that it amused her to consent to be . . . mastered when she knew that, in truth, the victory was hers? The true wanton is the one who submits.'

'Do you know something funny? You never s-stammered once when you were saying all that.'

'No more I did, though. Playback promises you're quite right. I was c-carried away.'

'Telling us what? That that whole stammering thing of yours is a conscious affectation, might it be?'

'It's the f-fruit of my b-bend sinister, s-someone told me. His name was Dexter. Is that the truth? Is it not? Delete "conscious"; it adds nothing. What's the other reason?'

'For what?'

'Asking me to tea. In a p-public p-platz? You advertised that your commission from the second most venal editor in London wasn't the main one. Are you hoping that someone in this less than smart company will go away and whisper about you, not to say "us"? The "main reason", you said, was c-commercial. What then was the supplementary one, or two?'

'I think there has to be something you're afraid of, and I'm curious to know what.'

'Blood,' Benedict Bligh said.

8

23. *Of Possible Relevance.* A picnic in a field, father, mother and daughter. In the background a church resembling that of Constable's Dedham. A sudsy froth of Hawthorn hedge runs along a lane at the wider side of the scene. The unbalanced proportions of the composition make it seem that the happy party risks being tilted into the void. The daughter, of four or five, is standing on her head as if to entertain the couple, who smile exclusively at each other. The child is not wearing knickers. The man has one hand inside the woman's shirt. With the other he is eating a hard-boiled egg. 48 x 32. Oil on board.

9

When Charlie picked up Camilla from the mews house her maternal great-aunt Sophie had left her, a few steps down from Alma Place, W8, the sky was tall and uncertain, the weather warm. He winced upwards and decided against unfolding the canvas roof over the Morgan. The sky grew leaden and mountainous as they headed along the A40 for Thame. It began to rain hard just after they had overtaken a suite of foreign lorries and a high bus, its misty windows lined with a frieze of old-age pensioners who waved in series.

Camilla said, 'Nothing like a good old-fashioned share-a-bang.'

Charlie said, 'Shall you mind terribly if we don't pull in and put the lid on at this point?'

Waterproofed with a yellow sou'wester and matching hat, Camilla shook her head. A mile or two before the Thame turn-off another Morgan came towards them over the top of a small rise.

'Bet you he gives us a wave.' Charlie timed his own wave to be just short of simultaneous with that of the other driver. 'I do rate antique courtesies. What finer provenance than to be a scion of a dying breed?'

'I do so love your bilge, bro, I really do.'

The rain was polishing their faces by the time they turned in between the tall gates of Potts. Shoulder-high steel mesh fences enclosed the woodland, with its underbrush of rhododendrons. Grey squirrels ran along with the car. As the Morgan rolled under the fawn stone portico of the early Georgian house ('mansionette' was Marcus's term for it), brother and sister leaned together for a wet kiss.

Charlie went to lift the canvas roof out of its fiddly housing.

'Bit late to do that now you're under cover, surely?' Lavinia Steele had opened the door, with her King Charles spaniel Liquorice Allsorts under one arm.

'I was going to budge it in case someone else was coming,' Charlie said.

'Everyone's here. Come in and get lubricated.' Lavinia had a kiss for Camilla and squeezed a smile for Charlie. 'And you calm down, Licky!'

Anya Djubenska clapped her hands together as brother and sister came through the double door of the L-shaped drawing-room. Not tall but well-proportioned, she was wearing a little black dress with a jagged jet necklace around her smooth, white neck. There was a matching jet bracelet on her left wrist. She had a thin, sharp, not quite straight nose, alabaster skin. The large breasts, faintly veined with blue, were handsomely sustained by the scoop of her neckline. Bright dark eyes were set on high cheekbones which her smile promoted. The hair was bronzy-red. Marcus's desire was manifest in the focus of his attention and his wish for hers. He expected Charlie to understand; and Charlie did.

Lavinia winced at the flicker of the electric lights and the almost immediate thunder. 'I do wish it wouldn't do that. We've got a Siamese cook. One loud flash and he's all set to run back to his wen or his wat or whatever it is they have.'

'Time for a top-up,' Brigadier Steele said, 'before all the lights go out and we can't find our way to the bottles.'

'Careful now, Tufty! You know what stormy weather does to you and alcohol.'

'Have I ever told you, Marsden, that I sometimes think it would've been better, in some regards, if I'd gone down with my ship?'

'I didn't know you were ever in command of one, sir.'

'I wasn't; that's why I didn't. Do you think Marcus is mine? I'm not all that sure. Depends on the light rather. Where did the dago lips come from? Imagine what I could've done with a pair of those.'

Lavinia said, 'He's supposed to go and see someone in London, but he keeps puttering it off. Meanwhile, don't drink any more, Tufts, not before we eat.'

'I don't know why you aren't the one to go to London, Vinny. Let me tell you something, Marsden, *entre nous*, but spread it about if you must. Viceroys, field-marshals, maharajahs of various sexes, papal nuncios, more than one, leaders of men of the greater or lesser potency, I've had occasion to raise my glass to, both in the line of duty and in pursuit of dreamless sleep.' It was not the first time that Charlie had heard Brigadier Steele rehearse the titles of his famous acquaintance, but the effusion of red and purple under and above his collar was of a richer hue than he had observed before. 'And not one of them, not one, until my dear wife stepped into the breach, has ever set fit to cast the smallest nasturtium on my capacity to hold liquor.'

A small brown person, buttoned to the throat in an umber cotton costume, was waiting in the doorway for the Brigadier to finish. He then said, 'Madam is served.'

'Dins!' Lavinia said. 'Now, if not sooner. See if we can beat the black-out, shall we, Licky?'

'Ah, the black-out,' the Brigadier said, taking Charlie's arm. 'Thereby hung a tale or three. The midnight rut between strangers has a quality no sanctioned coition can ever furnish. Vinny could probably tell you some stories about the Blitz which she's certainly never told me; apart from one figuring a character called Derek which seems to have gone on well after the All Clear.'

'Remind me again, Brigadier, what's the difference between a rajah and a maharajah?'

'Easy one: rajahs can only go on white squares; maharajahs can please themselves and often do. How's your father these days?'

'Largely in liquid form,' Charlie said.

'Nowadays she smells of dog,' the Brigadier said. 'Why is that such a good idea?'

Just before they reached the dining-room there was another volley of thunder. The electric lights hesitated and then went out. Even the candles on the dining table seemed to quiver in sympathy.

Anya clapped her hands again. 'Oh,' she said, 'I do love England so very, very much. It's so, so . . . naughty!'

10

She was kneeling on the rug at the side of a brass bedstead. Her folded clothes were on a straight chair, one of two bracketing the full mirror on the wall in front of the bed. Smooth upstretched arms reached across the silk coverlet. Her head was turned towards the bolster where a bell-push, on a long flex, was available. She lay there, flat, for some time. Then, not looking, she reached for the bell, as if for a delicacy. She held the plastic egg in her hand for a long moment, and she pressed the thingy.

The ring sounded some distance away. After a few minutes, she heard a door shut. Footsteps were heard to come up uncarpeted back stairs. There was a professional cough in the corridor before the door of the bedroom was opened.

'You rang, madam.'

'Yes, I did.'

'May we take it that madam is ready?'

'Yes, I am,' she said. 'Please.'

'Which do you want? First?'

'I leave the selection to him.'

'Thank you, madam.' The man took a step towards the door. 'How many?'

'You tell me.'

'Madam will have to wait a while longer.'

'With pleasure,' she said.

'Madam will stay exactly as she is now, won't she?'

'Of course.'

'We shall know if she moved.'

'She knows.'

'And madam is aware of the consequences.'

'Very.'

'Madam must do as she wishes.'

'Shall you be long?'

'We shall see, shan't we, madam?'

The man went out of the room. She sighed and waited. Then she heard him come back. He did what he always did, just the once, before he went out again.

She said, 'Thank you.'

11

Potts was a long, narrow Queen Anne dower-house. From the front door it was no more than eight yards to the french doors at the back. They gave on to the wide terrace that commanded a view of the croquet pitch, the unmarked, not yet mown tennis court and a two-acre field in which the Brigadier grazed his retired grey hunter, Monty (for Montmorency, never Montgomery, a four-letter man in the Brigadier's Overlord experience). The big house, on a site just over the horizon to the west, had burned down at the turn of the century and was never rebuilt. Potts summarized what no longer existed on the grand scale.

The breakfast room was on their left as Charlie and Camilla coincided on the stairs past the Dendy Sadler painting of a village attorney. A few steps lower down was Edmund Niemann's portrait of General Seaton Steele, one of the last men to have been able to buy a commission in the British Army. On the ground floor was a portrait of Florence Yealand, Lavinia's grandmother, painted (rather hurriedly, in Charlie's view) by Augustus John.

Warm smells from the buffet promised that the electric current had been restored in good time.

'Did you sleep, Charlesworth?'

'Like a top. Why do tops sleep?'

'It saves them worrying.'

'We're in luck. Kedgeree! We might even get a chuk-kah of croaks in if the weather holds.'

'Oh, it vill hold, I sink,' Camilla said.

'Yes, indeed,' Charlie said. 'Tell me: what does Marco see in her, do you suppose?'

'Well, she does have notable knobs on.'

'Yes, and also –'

Camilla put a finger to her lips. The louder and closer of the sets of approaching footsteps belonged to Marcus, who was fully dressed. He made a warning face as Anya's heels were heard to click and stop just short of the morning room. It sounded as if it required a deep breath for her to find the energy to come on in. When she did, she looked at neither of them. She seemed to blame Marcus that they were there at all. She wore no lipstick, no mascara; her eyes looked smaller. Even the breasts seemed downcast. Her head was banded in a red kerchief. No hair was visible.

Camilla said, 'Morning, Marcus. Morning, Anya.'

Marcus had collected a heated plate and was helping himself to the buffet. Anya selected the smallest sausage from the undercover possibilities.

Charlie poured himself more coffee. 'We were speculating whether we might not get some croquet in due course. I hope you're on.'

'Truth to tell,' Marcus said, 'we're off. Anya needs to get back to town in rather a rush.'

His soft words seemed to be enough to impel Anya to pick up the cup of black coffee he had poured and walk out of the room.

Marcus said, 'All right. If you must know, it's her head.'

'What's she got against aspirin?'

'Not that kind of head.'

'No? What kind of head is it exactly?'

'Not for me to divulge, Carlo.'

'Do we get guesses?'

'Many as you like. I remain sworn to secrecy.'

'And you're still not going to tell us?'

'It's not at all funny, that I can tell you.'

Marcus went out of the room. Camilla covered her mouth.

'Seems we shall have to croak on our own,' Charlie said.

12

She could hear footsteps on the back stairs. They slurred as they came to the door of the bedroom. Then they stopped. She waited for more than the usual number of minutes before the door was opened.

The man said, 'Is madam content?'

'She is.'

'Did she move?'

'As you can see.'

'When she was told not to.'

'Yes.'

'In knowledge of the consequences.'

'Of course.'

'And are we to proceed?'

'Yes.'

'Madam is going to say please, is she not?'

'Madam is. Please.'

'The tariff is doubled, the master has decided.'

'As you will.'

'All in good time. The master likes to look at madam.'

'As he wishes.'

'Madam will not move again, will she?'

'No.'

'Because she knows what it will mean, doesn't she?'

'She does.'

13

Theo's restaurant, in Elystan Street, a dozen yards up from Chelsea Green, was called 'The Gunroom'. Framed cases mounted on the walls carried flintlocks, muskets and antique shotguns. Charlie limped in, newly sun- and wind-burnt, leaning on a gnarled stick, after Easter leave at Méribel. He was carrying a brown paper parcel professionally tied with good old brown string.

Theo had had advice from Master Hicks on renovating the premises. A glass wall had been interposed between the dining area – with its irregular ruddy-and-blue carpet and discretely placed early Victorian tables with central pedestals – and the surgical kitchen where, in buttoned whites, toque tilted under the wide copper hood, Theo appeared to be blushing as he sowed herbs, fresh and dried, on steaks and fish cutlets ranged on the long slant of the grill.

Content for Theo to take his time, Charlie surveyed the visible diners. Those out of his eyeline were ensconced in buttoned blue velvet alcoves along the side walls. Slim waiters, in gondoliers' blue-striped tops, white lace-up espadrilles and bell-bottomed string-fastened white trousers, brought dishes from the service counter. Some plates were triangular, others square; the former black, the latter white. For the signature dessert, the dishes were of rectangular translucent glass, divided into twelve berths for their segregated complement of miniature crèmes brûlées, sorbets, tartes Tatin and profiteroles. The confusion of ancient and modern gave the place a discordant chic which had attracted favourable remark in the glossy press.

Theo wiped his hands and came through the portholed door at the side of the glass wall. Charlie held up his brown paper parcel with thumb and forefinger. 'As promised. Zu Zurich! Rifled, no doubt, from all the right schlosses.'

'Good snow?'

'Passable snow,' Charlie said. 'I was run over, since you're kind enough not to ask whatever happened to me, by a ponderous, rapidly transient Scandinavian with mercurial eyes. Claimed he didn't see me and waited not for an answer. Had a rendezvous to play chess with the Devil, probably.'

Theo was undoing the proffered package on the sole unoccupied table; close to the kitchen door, no one would to want to sit there, except as a last-minute unbooked favour. The inner wrapping parted to reveal a polished hardwood box, inlaid with a mother-of-pearl crest. A neat key, and its double, dangled from the keyhole on a wire loop. Once opened, the box could be seen to contain a pair of Teutonic duelling pistols aptly partitioned in claret lining. The stocks and barrels sported clever silver curlicues.

'His and hers, no doubt,' Charlie said. 'At a cursory count, Master Theobald, it looks to me as if my modest punt on your little caff was adequately well advised. You're certainly getting a few crocks dirtied.'

'So far so chock-a-block,' Theo said. 'Can't promise even the near or the dear an eight o'clock table between now and the end of the week after next.' Theo seemed to be making himself large and, in the casual process, contrived to hamper Charlie's sight of the occupants of a banquette recessed below two box-framed cases of belligerent cutlery. 'These beauties are over and above, Charles, truly.'

'Don't think ill of me because they're cheap at the price, will you?' Taking Theo's concealment of his customers as a prompt, Charlie was leaning to have a look just as Camilla's face, and new hair-do, came round the side of the banquette. Her face was cheek to cheek with the fat seat. A hand reached out and wiggled for his. When he took it, she pulled him towards her so that he could see that her previously hidden companion was Marcus Steele.

Charlie said, 'Well, well, I have been away, have I not? When did this happen? And what's become of – and I'm not thinking of Waring, although I was at prep school with one such – Madame Polska Poleska?'

'It's a long story.'

'Tell it. Some of it. What do the Yanks call them? Bullet points? The chairman's taken to asking for them at the bank.'

Marcus said, 'You remember her hair? Anya's?'

'Red stuff.'

'What happened was, it all came out.'

'The colour? So? Isn't it known to do that?'

Marcus said, 'The hair. That night at Potts. Lots of

it. The rest in due course and increasingly furious hand-fuls. Not a pretty sight. Consequence: she shut herself into 12A Albert Court, three mortise locks and two poodles, and that, basically, was that. Somehow her shame turned into my fault.'

'Can happen. You look wonderful, sister. On no account tell me why.'

'It's this new man I've got,' Camilla said. 'Xavier. For my hair. You'd never guess this was a wig, would you? Of course you wouldn't, because it isn't, but I've got one just like it, in case.'

'You could always lend it to the countess, if that's what she is.'

'Do you remember Harry Groves?'

'Should I?'

'The Jehu who brought Katya Lowell to Ferdy's party.'

'And took her away again, Bristol-fashion. His name escaped me.'

'Oh, by the way, someone's bought Ferdy's thriller-diller for a movie apparently. Many spondulicks. He's exceptionally unexcited.'

'Groves, of course! What about him?'

'He's been murdered.'

'Seriously?'

'Well, he's dead from it.'

'Why do I find that rather alarming?'

'That's between you and him, if that's who it's between.'

14

'Thank you.'

15

There was a narrow apron of slantwise parking spaces inside the iron fence along the front of Royalton House, across from the crematorium on the Harrow Road. The block of flats had Crittall windows and the economic elevation of dwellings designed, in 1936, for those who aspired to the middle class. A recent wooden plaque insisted that the parking was 'TENANTS ONLY'. Charlie left the Morgan, roof up, doors locked, in a 'STRICTLY TRADESMEN' space adjacent to a modest door labelled 'STAFF ONLY'. He walked along and opened one of the glassed double doors into the main foyer. A uniformed porter, in dark-blue brass-buttoned tunic, thick black stripes down the trouser legs, cap on the counter, was sorting the morning post.

Charlie said, 'I hope it's all right, chief, but I'm by way of subbing for a tradesman.'

'Meaning?'

Charlie was leaning on the counter. 'I've put my van where it says . . .' The hand he raised to indicate where he had parked the motor uncovered a pound note. 'I have something of a favour to ask you.'

'You never know.'

Charlie said, 'Harry Groves.'

'Doesn't live here any more.'

'Tactfully put. I know. All the same . . .'

'Not a copper, are you? Or a reporter?'

'Nil returns in both columns, sergeant-major, I shouldn't wonder. I'm one of the idly curious.'

'Colour-sergeant, sir. Cherry-picker, me. What were you in, made you say that?'

'How about the Buffs? Not in the war, of course.'

'Very wise of you, sir, from what I saw of it.'

'Were you around when it . . . happened? Upstairs, I mean.'

'Torremolinos, me, at the time.'

'Still the place I think it is?'

'In the R & R department? Very much so, I should imagine, sir. Something for everyone, as they say.'

'Mostly the same thing, in my brief experience. What was he like? Mr Groves.'

'Had money, no shortage. But he wasn't no gentleman, not like yourself. Truth to tell, sir, I'm rather surprised –'

'Truth to tell *you*, I saw him but the once. He wore a suit . . . with a lot of . . .'

'Cupboards full of 'em, sir, he had; suits. Most of 'em on what someone such as yourself might term the saloon-bar side . . .'

'One can't have everything. But he does seem to have had pretty well everything else. Regular, I presume, were you?'

'Only thirty years.'

'His flat. Anyone living in it at the moment?'

'He still gets letters, though. Two came this morning. I bung them in there for want of anywhere better. If the police ever want to see anything, that's where it'll be. My impression, they're in no sort of a hurry. Case of a dead end in more senses than one.'

'You weren't on your way up there, by any chance?'

'I might well be shortly.'

'Might we shorten that, possibly?' Charlie's hand was again on the counter. When he lifted it this time there was a fiver underneath.

'No need for that, sir.'

'That's rather what I like about it. Unlike taxes.'

The porter unlocked a drawer in his kiosk and took out a wide hoop of keys. 'They nailed down all the letter-boxes on the individual flat doors because people used to get things put through them.'

The plastic-lined lift took them to the third floor. The porter looked at the fan of unmarked keys and picked out the right one for 317. Two turns and they were in. The furniture in Harry Groves's flat accorded with the date of the building. The living-room had a beige couch with matching tasselled armchairs. A three-leaved mirror, each curved section in a silvered surround, hung over the mantelpiece on a chromium chain. There were cold plastic coals along the bottom of the two-burner electric fire. Bookcases extended on each side of the fireplace. Sidelong magazines were stacked on the shelves, wide gaps between them; there were few bound books. Charlie noticed *The Cruel Sea*, *Forever Amber*, *They Fought Alone* and *Les Amours de Caroline Chérie*. The ornaments in the room looked to be of the kind acquired in airports at the end of foreign holidays. A furry off-white rug was spread on the beige moquette in front of the fireplace. There were no pictures on the walls.

'Did he have women up here?'

'Did he not!'

'The bedroom. Might I see it?'

'Through here.'

The buttoned green bed-head appeared bruised, whether by heads or feet. The bow-legged dressing table was painted white and gold and had a matching chair and three-leaved mirror. Another mirror, full-length, on the front of the walnut wardrobe, faced the bottom of the wide bed. Two double sets of metal-framed windows looked on to the Harrow Road.

'These women. Any favourites at all?'

'There was only the one he ever opened the lift door for that I noticed.'

'Did she ever arrive by herself? Tall and slim, with dark brown hair.'

'And quite the lady. Always said good evening. Sure you're not a copper?'

'I take it she did, sometimes. Come alone.'

'She never looked better, truth to tell, sir, than when she did that. As if she was going to a very special sort of party. Not that Mr Groves ever gave parties. Men and women . . . generally came separately.'

'But not . . . one at a time, necessarily.'

'No, sir.'

'The last time you ever saw the lady we're talking about, how long was that before you . . . went to Torremolinos?'

'Quite a few weeks, sir. I didn't keep a log, but some

time. I was conscious she'd stopped because . . . she was quite a looker.'

'Who do you think killed him?'

'Not the lady, I don't imagine. He did have friends, if friends they were.'

'Men? Who seemed as though . . .?'

'. . . They knew what they were about, let's say. They none of them ever asked me which number Mr Groves was. Always went straight on up. As if they was expected. I don't recall any of 'em ever coming on his own.'

'He looked to me like a man who knew how to take care of himself.'

'And other people, sir, if you know what I mean.'

'I very well may. Which is what . . .'

'I agree with you, sir. There must've been more than one of them killed him. More than two, if I'm any judge, and they wanted to be on the safe side. No one heard a thing, is what they tell me. Bathroom was a bit special, if you'd care for a squint.'

The thick door to the bathroom fitted into a hermetic steel frame. The floor, walls and ceiling were covered with white tiles. The oval bathtub was big enough for two or three people. The fittings were modern. The original window had a new shiny black Venetian blind over the bubbly frosted glass. There was a mirror in the ceiling above the bath.

'How was he killed exactly, sergeant-major, and where?'

'He was in the tub and, although I didn't see him

personally, he was apparently . . . let's say suffocated. In a plastic bag, with chemical residue in it, so I happened to hear one of the coppers say.'

Charlie said, 'He could look up and watch himself dying.'

'We'll leave it at that, sir, if you don't mind.'

When they were back downstairs and the porter returned to his kiosk, Charlie discovered another five pounds under his hand.

'Not often we get a gentleman such as yourself in here. One odd thing I do know about Mr Groves. He was bilingual, if you know what I mean.'

'Bilingual. Was he indeed? In the how's-your-father department?'

'Not all that likely, in view of all the women what went up and came down. But you never know, do you? I was meaning he spoke French as well as English.'

'That explains . . . his reading matter, possibly.'

'He got letters with French stamps on them from time to time; gave me a quite a few of them. For my grandson's collection.'

'Nice of him.'

'One or two unused.'

'The Bristol,' Charlie said. 'What happened to that? His car.'

'Must've gone back where it came from. He told me he always rented his motors, sir. Told me it was safer.'

'Than what, would that be?'

'That he didn't say, sir. Not the talkative type, exactly.'

16

2. *And the Referee Points to the Spot.* A woman in a white, transparent cotton shift, on one shoulder and off the other, recalling a blue-period Picasso, is seated in front of a 1930s' triple mirror in which she sees the reflections, as if they were her own, of a quite different woman; a bare-chested man with a shaven head in a sleeveless white vest; and a young girl, her chin resting on a closed fist. 60 x 44. Oil on board.

17

Almost prone in the deep *bergère* chair which Marcus had elected to leave behind, Charlie was at ease in his brocade dressing-gown, over city trousers, feet in black house-shoes. The *Evening News* lay across his knees, open at the City page. On top of it was a short stack of typewritten foolscap; its enumerated sections and alphabetically denoted sub-sections bore plastic tabs in primary colours.

When the street bell rang Charlie put the foolscap pages aside and resumed the *Evening News*. The bell rang again, with a familiar double urgency. He said, 'Oh, all right then', and walked to the window, pausing to untangle a ball of brown string from the half-open desk drawer. A key was double-knotted to the loose end. He opened the window, leaned out to confirm who was there and unravelled the string until the key clinked at street level and could be snaffled and used to open the street door. When the string was jerked, Charlie reeled it up again. He was waiting at the top of the long stairs as Marcus and Camilla climbed and climbed.

'To what do I owe it?' Charlie said. 'Not that it isn't welcome.'

'We wanted you to be the first to ker-now,' Camilla said.

'Ker-now what, might that be? Ah! Got it: you're wearing socks.'

Camilla was flashing a pair of Argyll socks over her nylons; Marcus was not wearing socks at all.

'She had cold feet,' Marcus said.

'But she did it just the same.'

'Only because Marcus asked me nicely.'

'We're going to get married,' Marcus said.

' If I'm the first to ker-now, it follows as the day the night that there's someone who doesn't.'

'That's not the least reason we've come round, to be entirely honest.'

'To be entirely honest is almost always a beastly reason to come round.'

'Presumably you've guessed.'

'That you want me to play Uncle Charles and shout the bad news through the Countess Votsit's letter-box and then run away. Or is there more?'

Marcus said, 'Would you mind terribly if I used your bog?'

'Still where you left it. And probably in much the same state. Do you want a drink or anything, sis?' Charles said. 'He can't have been nervous, can he? I do hope you know what you're doing, if that's what you're doing.'

'Oh, Charlesworth, I do hope I don't.'

'I love Marcus dearly . . .'

'Snap, darling, totally, at this stage.'

'. . . But I don't need to tell you –'

'You need not to. I know already. I rather like that part. What's important is, he keys me like a bastard. I do rate second helpings. About . . . um . . . her countess-ship, please be nice. I'll bet she could be a terror with a hat-pin at the opera or somewhere like that.'

'Being nice is my biggest failing. Does he . . . do what m'tutor almost gave him the chuck for doing with Bubbles B?'

'Only when I ask him nicely. And don't you dare mention any similarity between thee and me.'

Charlie embraced her. 'You are a lucky girl. I hope. Marcus is a charmer and charmers can . . . get away with murder, can't they?'

'Second thoughts, I could do a small voddy, if you've got one handy. With a squeeze.'

He poured the drinks. Marcus and Camilla drank them and then they looked at their watches.

'I know,' he said, 'if 'twere done and all that. 12A, am I right?'

'Albert Court. Third floor. You are a brick.'

'Explains why you're dropping me,' Charlie said.

18

4. *First Wicket Down.* A pale-blue china cup and saucer. The handle of the cup has been broken off. In the saucer, where the handle might have fallen, is a caterpillar, of the species 'Sleepy Sulphur' (*Abaeis Nicippe*), crooked in the form of a question mark. Oil on board. 32 x 22.

19

The studio was furnished in black and white. The unplastered brick walls were whitewashed. A large sofa, which could be folded out into a double bed, was covered in black leather; a wide flokati carpet in front of it. The wall behind the bed was a black mirror. On the white wall facing the bed a series of white square canvases were framed in black; black in white. The two windows on to the cobbled mews had stainless-steel Venetian blinds.

'Take off anything you want to.'

'This isn't at all what I expected of you.'

'Then again . . . you were about to say . . .'

'The unexpected is just what I should have expected; and all that. Some of it. How can a place have personality and no personality at all?'

'Do you want some champagne?'

'Has your wife ever seen it?'

'Why should she not?'

'But has she?'

'Suze's got nothing to do with what happens here. She knows that.'

'That's what she's got to do with it, in other words.'

'You're a c-clever girl, sometimes, and you want me to know it. Why?'

'Do you suppose she doesn't know what you do when you're here?'

'Do you know? Or are you hoping to find out? Or fearing? Is fear a kind of hope? Think about it. If you want to. Are you imagining that I shall show signs of shame? Champagne! How can we be sure what we hope for? Relief can be a disappointment, can't it? Like not being wanted on voyage. Cheers.'

'If you say so. Is it part of your pleasure that you know she knows and doesn't want to know all at the same time?'

'No,' he said. 'No.'

'You say that quickly and then you say it slowly. Indicating what?'

'She knows that I love her,' he said. 'I love her and that's . . .'

'Yes?'

'. . . Why my idea of pleasure has nothing to do with what she and I have together.'

'And if you had to choose one or the other?'

'I've chosen. Both.'

'You sacrifice love for pleasure.'

'Hers or mine?'

'Does she have a lover? She does.'

'You look as if you know and as if you hope that I don't. Yes, she does. A photographer, isn't he? Which is amusing, if that's your idea of amusement. My pleasure is not unfaithful; and her infidelity . . . if you want to put it that way . . .'

'. . . Is not pleasurable?'

'Was I going to say that?'

'But you do hope it.'

64

'Might it not be her form of . . . acquiescence? An act of generosity, I sometimes think.'

'And when you're not thinking that?'

'Generosity and something else; vanity, probably. A beautiful woman is entitled to that. She couldn't love me if she was faithful to me, in the technical sense. What she does pander to is her pride. And here comes generosity again. Deceit that doesn't deceive. Because it also allows me to love her without falsehood. Falsehood is worse than infidelity, especially in the cant sense.'

'Can you really love one woman and yet . . .?'

'Is there any other way? You want love to be something rare and fine, oh, and so it is, so it is; but it can also be . . . something expressed in – how shall we say? – transgression, then all may join in! The human lot and his wife, too; the one who looks back. I allow her that possibility gladly, in principle, however much it may pinch in sorry practice.'

'The music goes round and round.'

'Don't you find?' he said. 'The thing being to avoid it going flat. The moment of rarest pleasure, however frequently one contrives to enjoy it, lies in crossing the line. The clever do it, one way or another, with more finesse than the profane crowd. We few, happy or no, must trump mortality as best we can. By playing Faust and louche.'

'Oh dear,' she said, 'I'm making you try. How fortunate for your reputation that we're alone!'

'You're hoping to vex me.'

'And am I succeeding?'

'It's a flattering ambition. In truth, however, you're pleasing me more than you know. And you know it, don't you? So what can it be you would like me to do to you?'

She said, 'Do you like them to enjoy what you do to them?'

'Do what?'

'You know what you do.'

'Tell me,' he said, 'what you imagine it to be.'

'What do you use?'

'Varies, doesn't it? No scorpions, though. Pleasure and surprise are part of the same recipe. The sex likes to be surprised and doubly so when they are surprised at what surprises them in themselves.'

'Has she ever asked you for details, your wife?'

'She doesn't need to. I have reason to think she's seen my notes.'

'Does she ever feel deprived, do you suppose?'

'I used to wish I could give her that pleasure,' he said. 'But she's too . . .'

'Proud? Cold?'

'She will think of afterwards. These things can't be enjoyed if one does that. There is nothing tragic in sex, nothing, still less domestic; and everything that is comic. To smile at a woman when you have done the things I like to do and have her smile back, because – although she may never say as much out loud – she likes one to do them; there is the triumph over mortality, the humour that no god can ever enjoy.'

'One!'

'You have it. I am the instrument, I have no illusions there.'

'Unless that's your illusion.'

'I suspect you've played this game before. Are you getting a little heat?'

'How many women do you bring here and won't . . . let you do those things?'

'None,' he said. 'Or why would they consent to come? Are you intending to be different? Do you want to be? Imagine going too far. Imagine not doing so, and what you will have missed. That fine line, where is it, Mistress T?'

20

27. *Portrait of an Artist.* The body of a white female on a stretcher laid in a rural lane. A blue coat covers the body, but the feet are uncovered. One wears a blue low-heeled shoe, the other is bare and has red-painted toenails. 32 x 24. Acrylic on paper.

21

There was a yapping of poodles as soon as Charlie touched the bell of Anya's flat. He waited and then touched it again. He backed from the door so that she could see, through the spy-hole he was sure she was behind, that he was flashing nothing nastier than a sheaf of mint magazines. He heard locks being undone. The door came open an inch or two.

'Charlie Marsden. We met at Potts. Don't remember if you don't want to.'

The brass chain was unholstered and there she was, in a cotton housecoat covered with blown roses, pink slippers with white woolly lining. Her face was cold-creamy; red and black bandanna tight around her head.

'Brought you these.' Charlie held out the magazines. 'In case you needed refreshment. On no account put them in water.'

'I know very well why you're here.'

'Like Havelock, I was sent to raise the siege.'

'If you want to come in, come in. I have nothink to offer you.'

The drawing-room had a wide bay window. Charlie could see the sweep of steps leading up to the back of the Albert Hall. She let him stand there among the polished furniture. The poodles sat at her feet and looked at him.

'You, of course, are very 'appy,' she said. 'He is a catch and a half. For that sister of yours. Marcovitch.'

'Catch, is he?'

'You and he were at school togezzer, he told me.'

'Can happen with Englishmen, unless they're very, very careful. Might just be a case of who caught whom, if you care to read the runes.'

'Havelock? Who is Havelock?'

'See under "Lucknow, siege of". Ancient history. Not worth pursuing.'

Anya continued to be a model of implacable bereavement. Charlie reached and placed the magazines adjacent to her on the arm of a two-seater couch. He could not think of what further to say, and it was too far to the door to go without saying anything. The blackness of her eyes seemed muted. Her head seemed smaller, too.

After an extended silence, Charlie said, 'Oh, look here, ducky. I didn't pull your bloody hair out or whatever happened to it. Red, white or blue, whatever it is now, what's it got to do wiz me? Not a great deal.'

Anya reared back, as if gathering enough breath to scream at him, and then she was smiling under her scowl. 'Beast!'

'That's better,' he said. 'Possibly. Who's the beast?'

'I knew,' she said. 'Of course I knew. As soon as he began to be very, very kind to me on ze telephone.' She raised a hand to her forehead. 'And then, the second time, he told me someone had come to the door and he had to go, sorry.'

'Try this for size, Anyushka: you've basically had a rather lucky escape. Seeing as you're a foreign make, chances are Marcus would've chipped your paintwork and then passed you on to the nearest ghastly. Pray God, if you can stretch to it, he doesn't do likewise to my sister. As for you, box on, I should. In the *fra tempo*, allow me to advise you of one thing, of possibly capital moment: it don't matter a toss. Your hair. In terms of your push-me pull-you powers.'

'I do not have a single blade,' she said. 'Not one. After what the wheezy teaser did to me.'

'Really? Show me. When I tell you to. Because I bet you, you look . . . novel!'

'You, too, are a beast.'

'Beasts and beauties, old, old story. I'm prepared to bet, heavily, that it doesn't matter a toss. Truth to tell, I can't wait to be right. Or wrong. Take it off and we'll see.'

Anya looked down at the sedentary poodles. '*Allez-vous* out,' she said. '*Tous les deux* of you!'

They skittered on the parquet between the possibly Persian carpet and the similar mat in front of the drawing-room door, and then they were gone. Anya shut the door and returned to stand, differently, in front of Charlie. She raised her hands to the knot at the back of the bandanna, face more vulnerable, and younger, for the now arrested movement.

'Yes, I did,' he said. 'Ask for it. So . . .'

She loosened the bandanna and peeled it, in no hurry, from her naked scalp. 'Now you can see. I am no

71

longer a woman. Wizout my clowning glory, I am no more than . . . a wedge-ettable.'

He looked at her with an unexpected hardness. He took her by the hunched shoulders and straightened her up and kissed the top of her head. He was surprised by how much of her polished scalp his lips could embrace. Then he tasted one of her ears.

'Take it all bloody off,' he said. 'Let's have a proper look at you while we're at it, if we are.'

She said, 'I must warn you, dear: I am bald only in ze head department. Not . . . elsewhere. No laughing.'

'I shall never laugh,' Charlie said, 'unless you laugh first.'

'Oh! A gentleman!'

'If only for fear of your *mitteleuropan* hat-pin.'

His stance made a feature of his desire. After a watchful moment, she let the housecoat slip off her shoulders and slide down her white body until she was a vertical odalisque, with a glistening bush, standing in a rumple of cotton.

'So zere you are, dear. You are a gentleman and I, you can see . . . I am a lady. Hat-pin?'

He might have been angry with her, the way he looked. He hardly knew what he felt, only what he wanted. 'Never mind.' Desire stood in for anything else he might be feeling. So did it, he could see, with her. 'If only Edouard Manet could see you now!'

'Damaged goods,' she said, 'I am. Or you would never have dared. Am I right? I don't need to ask. And I don't care. So . . .'

She turned and bent double and there she was again: an inverted face smiling at him from between sinewy thighs. When she had straightened up, she said, 'Yes, as you don't ask, I tell you, yes, at one time I was: going to be a dancer. But my bust grew too important. So what do you say?'

'That I find you an item of brazen symmetry. Tyger, tyger, I may well call you.'

'And will I come?'

'Time will tell. As it only too often does.'

She said, 'We will be honest, yes?' He smiled at the way she pronounced the aitch.

'Honest as the day is lonje,' he said.

'And I will make you as 'appy as I know 'ow, and I do know 'ow! One thing I ask: you will never bite me, please. I hate to be black and blue. Blue is such a bad colour for me, dear.'

'You studied ballet.'

'You love it, yes?'

'Provided there's no surfeit of wobbly cods. And I don't terribly rate intervals.'

'Zen we have no intervals, dear. Not a one.'

She stepped clear of the hoop of discarded garments, shucked the slippers and stood on his shoes for better access to his lips. It was a new delight, Charlie discovered, to be dressed and to kiss a woman who was naked.

'And now', she said, 'I toot your flute for you, yes?'

22

On the six-to-eight-thirty evening of the Private View of Recent Work by Katya Lowell at the Rollo Farber Gallery in Motcomb Street, Anya was still wearing her head in a bandanna, but it was black and white now.

1. *Aubade.* A nocturnal view of a vividly lit suburban villa; opaque glass beacons flare on each side of the front door. Three men in hats and long coats, quiet shoes, confer under a street lamp, down to the left. Their shadows, and those of other elements in the picture, fall in a direction in contradiction to what would normally be appropriate to the position of the lamps. 44 x 28. Oil on board.

'I spent sick-sick-six months in New York and uns-s-similar places, and the only occasion on which I t-totally unpacked my s-suitcase was for the d-delectation of HM Cuss-Toms and X-eyes, who expected the worst and proved head-scratchingly disappointed to discover me c-clean as a b-bristol.' Benedict Bligh was wearing a black corduroy suit, with one of his frilly-fronted shirts, no tie, a black Balkan Sobranie cigarette between improbable fingers. 'I positively c-craved to be found to have something concealed in my c-crevices. Walking free is a dull form of exercise. Remember Meursault.'

Doris Vreeland said, 'Who the fuck is Merso?'

'A character who greeted the execration of the crowd as what you, my pineapple upside-down cake, would never call the *sacre*. He went to the scaffold with the same *morgue* as his creator did to Stockholm.'

Félix Kalpakian said, 'How is it you manage to turn up absolutely everywhere, Benedict, and still retain a reputation for being hard to get?'

Doris Vreeland said, 'Or is it hard to get hard, do I hear from a reliable sauce?'

'The very q, *mon cher* Félix, that I was about to put to you. No wonder they call you "*un peu partout*"!' The virtuoso pianist and sometime conductor wore a big felt hat and a wide woollen cape, but he was indeed a short man. 'T-truth is, as has just been vividly illustrated by the ostrich to your left, my search for the grail will end when I arrive at a p-party to which drum-beating, ball-breaking feminists have been denied access. What a clever one that Tamsin p-person is, to be late for me!'

'You flatter yourself, Benedict.'

'It's a living, d-dear adhesive D-Doris, of a kind unavailable to the – do I hear? – no longer commissioned lickety-split, not even by posy Rosie?'

'Fuck you, Benedict.'

'Improbable if I see you coming.'

18. *Nu de Dos*. A sloping terrace of two-storeyed artisans' dwellings with a Bristol parked in front of one of many severely pollarded plane trees. 40 x 32. Acrylic on board.

Rollo Farber was standing beside Charlie. 'What, I wonder, would m'tutor say if he could see us now?'

'Piggers? Make an arse, probably. It never took much. Wykhamist, wasn't he?'

'Never got over it. I do like her paint, don't you?'

'How well do you know her?'

'Katya? Not at all well, truth to tell, if I must. But then who does? She's quite a peremptory person. She comes and goes with very little in between. She knows what she wants. And nothing else at all does she want.'

'She knows you like that, presumably.'

'I do rate a perfectionist. She never suffers me to see anything until it's exactly as she means it to be.'

'Why is she not at the receipt of custom?'

'I thought she was. And, lo!, she is!'

Katya Lowell was standing in the goal-sized archway leading to the back of the gallery: Prussian-blue high-heeled shoes, black stockings, a long-sleeved silvery-blue close-fitting dress with a dark-blue belt, no jewellery except for tiny pearl earrings. The dark hair was lifted from her neck and contained, at the back, in a loose bun with no visible support. Fugitive curls, silvered by the top light, emphasized the slim whiteness of her neck.

6. *The Artist's Mother.* A grey, fluted dustbin, the black plastic lid not quite straight, under a spreading fig tree on which some bulbous purple fruits and a few large and yellowing leaves remain. Acrylic on paper. 38 x 22.

9.   *Eurydice* (*detail*). The entrance to Belsize Park Underground Station. There is a flower-stall adjacent to the railings but no one in attendance. Acrylic on board. 38 x 32.

5.   *Departure for Cythera*. A bedroom with stippled off-white walls. A chair with casters on the claw-and-ball feet in front of a mirror. On the chair a roll of camera tape. In the mirror, which might be expected to reflect the contents of the room, can be seen a little girl, pink bows on her plaits, in a toy car in a yellow field of rape. Acrylic on paper. 40 x 28.

Anya said, 'Forgive me saying so, darlingk, but . . .' She showed Charlie her watch.

Tamsin Fairfax was coming in, unhurriedly, as they went out into Motcomb Street.

Charlie said, 'He was afraid you weren't coming.'

Tamsin said, 'No, he wasn't.'

'Benedict.'

'I know who. Afraid doesn't come into it. *Experta crede!*'

'You quondam classicists do rub it in,' Charlie said. 'And how rarely one feels better for it afterwards! Taxi!'

Charlie and Anya left the theatre, as usual, at half-time. While they climbed the steps from Prince Consort Road, where the cabbie had dropped them, to the entrance of 9–16 Albert Court, a concert at the Albert Hall was reaching its conclusion. The first few members of the audience were already sneaking out while the applause was still going on. They came down the broad steps in furtive triumph as Charlie and Anya reached the high white entrance of the flats.

Charlie sat on the double sofa waiting while Anya fed the poodles. She came in at last, with clean hands, shut the drawing-room door, drew the curtains and stood in front of him. His hands were behind his head, which was almost down on the seat, legs extended in front of him. She pressed off her shoes and began to undress. Soon, but without haste, she was naked except for the black-and-white bandanna.

'Take it off, Anyuska. When I tell you.'

She smiled during what was now the ritual of undoing the tortoiseshell clasp at the back before she scarfed the bandanna around her hand and wrist.

'Didn't I tell you?' he said. 'Nanny was right. Not every time, fortunately. Just look at you, though! You look positively . . . complete!'

She turned her back to him, bent down and looked at him from between her thighs. 'Come and kiss ze little tweetie in ze bush!' He slid forward, on to his knees, shins on the carpet behind him. 'Naughty!'

23

17. *Will There Be Anything Else?* An antique walnut Windsor chair with a crinoline stretcher. A purple dress is laid across the seat over one arm of the chair, and drapes on to the floor. A black patent-leather belt hangs over the dressed arm of the chair and there are two bracelets, one gold, one silver, on the seat. Also a roll of masking tape. Oil on canvas. 32 x 40.

There was a red sticker at the bottom right corner of the title card.

Charlie changed his angle of vision and frowned, as if he hoped to crack a code. On the morning after the private view, the Rollo Farber gallery had no other civilians in it. Rollo himself was beyond the arch at the back, being businesslike with another dealer. *Will There Be Anything Else?* was one of a few canvases framed and glassed in the antique style.

22. *Don't Mention It.* In a field of wild flowers, bounded by a hawthorn hedge, a prepubertal girl, with long fair hair, wearing a short cotton vest. One hand between her legs, she is holding one of her feet close to the side of her face, as if it were a telephone receiver. Oil on board. 22 x 28.

The other dealer shook hands with Rollo, collected

his loose umbrella and went out into the dry morning. Rollo stood a few yards behind Charlie.

Charlie said, 'Why is it, Rollo, that it has the effect it does?'

'That being?'

'Perhaps it doesn't on you. It does on me. And it does seem, alas, that I'm not the only one.' Charlie indicated the red sticker next to *Will There Be Anything Else?* 'Comes of being in too much of a hurry the other night to go to that play Benny B. promised was "all sauce and no goose". He does have a nose.' They stood for a minute, not side by side, in front of *Will There Be Anything Else?*

Rollo said, 'What I value is that there isn't the faintest sniff in her work of that very dull dog mass appeal.'

Charlie said, 'Look here, Rollers, I accept that it's not normally done, but might I possibly be told who bought it?'

'No.'

'Any good saying please?'

'I did once have occasion, if memory serves, to administer stripes to you for doing things which were not normally done.'

Charlie stared at *Will There Be Anything Else?* quite as if he were looking Rollo in the eye, even though the gallery owner was standing a pace behind him. Then, with accuracy and force, he pivoted and bolo-punched Rollo's floral waistcoat just below the fourth button down. Rollo fell to the recently waxed floor and gasped and rolled about a bit. When he sat up and drew breath, Charlie offered him a hand. 'All right, Rollers?'

'I forgot you boxed, damn you. Bloody thug really, aren't you?'

'The trouble with memory is that its service can be unduly selective. The left can be followed by a right, you may now remember. You can, on the other hand, rely on me not to sneak.'

'His name's Jarvis Green, you total appendage.'

'All I wanted to know.'

Charlie walked up through Lowndes Square, across Knightsbridge and into the park, then down to Grosvenor Square and into Brook Street. He guessed that he might find Ferdy Plant at the Savile Club; and so he did. They went into the card room beyond the bar and played some backgammon, while three sad members were hoping for a fourth at bridge.

Charlie waited till Ferdy was almost a hundred points up, at a nominal ten bob a hundred, and then he said, 'Jarvis Green, Ferds. Know anything about him at all?'

'Nothing savoury. Not somebody one's likely to find in choirs and places where they sing. Why?'

'He happens to own a picture I rather fancy.'

'That all?'

'Where might I bump into him by happy chance?'

Ferdy said, 'Accept a double?'

'Don't I always, except when I don't?'

Ferdy shook and rolled the dice and said, 'That'll teach me! Now I shall have to open my legs.'

'Rich, I assume.'

'As such people often are. Do you still play poker at all?'

'How about another double,' Charlie said, 'seeing as how it's a friendly game? Always assuming a flush still beats a straight.'

'He runs quite a hot school, verging on do-not-touch. If you fancy that kind of outing. You'll need more than a little luck, I'm told, not to mention some tin.'

'Camilla's pregnant. Did she tell you?'

'Marcus did. Nothing to do with him, apparently.'

'Really? Are you sure? Does he mind?'

'In the sense that it was all her idea.'

'I do hope little sis knows who she's doing. Re Jarvis, can you alert somebody to my . . . wish to . . . test his waters?'

'I likewise hope you know what you're doing, Charlie Marsden.'

'Possibly best I don't, but I can't resist finding out. Whose turn to propose a double?'

'What are you, Charlie, drunk? Mine, and I'm not going to.'

24

25. *I Say Unto One, Go, And He Goeth*. A woman in winter clothes is walking along a rough country road at dusk. In her right hand she holds out a lantern in which a young naked girl is caged. The girl holds a small torch which shines on the road ahead. The *mise-en-scène*, but not the style, recalls an early work of Vincent Van Gogh. Oil on canvas. 36 x 30.

25

Jarvis Green's chauffeur pressed Charlie's bell and then returned to the metallic green Corniche that fortune had allowed him to park in Beaufort Street. Charlie came down, a few minutes later, in a dark-blue suit, white shirt, old school tie. His hair had been shampooed and cut at his usual place in Jermyn Street with instructed severity. His Chelsea boots struck a decidedly raffish note, the decision being Charlie's: a poker night in north London was not an occasion on which to be too uniform a gentleman.

The chauffeur was out on the pavement again in time to open the door for Charlie. Jarvis Green was alone in the back of the Corniche. He was in his late forties. The silk of his greeny-black Italian suit gleamed rather. The graph-paper shirt had a button-down collar. He slid some papers into a cellophane sleeve and holstered them in the briefcase at his feet. At the same time he reached out a pale hand. 'Welcome aboard.' The made-to-measure black shoes had leather flanges across the instep, fastened by silver buckles. 'Wagons roll, Cater, in your own time.'

Jarvis Green's dark brown hair was clipped against his scalp. His glasses had a straight plastic bar across the top, steel rims below. Charlie had never seen a man who looked more like a passport photograph. Face regular and expressionless, Jarvis Green sat, with one hand on the tassel in the corner, and said nothing until Cater was driving down Maida Vale. He continued to look out of the window as he said, 'You buy a lot of pictures, I gather.'

'Truth to tell,' Charlie said, 'I've never bought a one.'

'I was given to understand that you had quite a collection.'

'My walls happen to be all pretty well dressed already.'

'You had things in the family.'

'A few.'

'I got it as a present for my wife, the one you were . . . interested in. You'd have to talk to her about it, if you're really serious.'

'If she wouldn't find that . . . intrusive.'

'She might welcome it.' They halted at a red light in Kilburn High Road, just short of the State cinema. Jarvis Green said, 'Have you ever seen any of her films? She used to be Shona Sage.'

'I remember Shona Sage. From the Regal at Oxford. Rather vividly.'

'That's who she used to be.'

They drove closer to Pinner than Charlie had ever been before and then the Corniche branched off along a leafy suburban avenue. The well-spaced houses had in-and-out gates and commodious garages. Cater turned down another tree-lined road which proved to be a cul-de-sac. The Corniche halted at the mouth of a driveway. When Cater did something electric both wings of a crested metal gate yielded way. The name of the house – Villa Verde – split in half and one word went each way as the gates receded. A white Mercedes 500 SEL, a blue Lagonda, an open Alfa Romeo 2800 Spider and a black Cadillac Coupe de Ville were parked in front of the large glazed-white-brick house. Charlie could see two powerful black motorcycles under the tilted horizontal door of one of the double garages.

The three-storey house had many leaded windows in steel frames. Its shiny green-tile roof was punctuated by half-a-dozen dormers. Flame-shaped glass lamps glowed, unnecessarily, on each side of the white arch over varnished double doors at the top of a short stack of five semicircular stone steps. 'Home sweet home,' Jarvis Green said.

26

11. *Nursery School.* A modern city office, with strict metal and black leather furniture. The wide desk under Venetian-blinded windows has a pen set, metal ruler, black-handled scissors and letter-knife, a range of telephones. Averted photographs of happy people, some on skis, are half visible, compressed in rimless plastic frames on clear plastic pedestals. Ink and charcoal. 32 x 60.

27

By three-fifteen in the morning the air in Jarvis Green's recreation room was layered with used cigar smoke. The oval poker table had wooden scallops let into the mahogany margin to accommodate each of seven players' effects. The stretched green baize in the middle was strewn with spent chips and a jumble of cards, some face up, others not. Low-backed captain's-style armchairs had been pushed here and there by players who had already settled up and left.

Charlie, still in jacket and tie, and Jarvis Green, now in shirt-sleeves, collar unbuttoned, were smoking Romeo y Julietas. In the wide shadows at the back of the room was a full-size billiard table, a pool table and a veteran pin-table adjacent to it. Brazen women in tartan shirts with pistols and Stetsons were painted on the lit glass scoreboard.

Charlie's manner and expression, as he signed a sizeable cheque, would have been appropriate to a modest winner. He handed it across as if it were his subscription to a rare club.

Jarvis said, 'I had the cards.'

'So I noticed.'

'Win some, lose fewer. The only recipe for a quiet life. A famous name told me that.'

Charlie said, 'Do you have children?'

'One. Jason. He's going to Oxford.'

'Really? Which college?'

'Not sure,' Jarvis Green said. 'He's only eleven at the moment. I may have to found one for him. Would you like to see my wife?'

'Is this quite the time?'

'Presents no sort of a problem.'

Jarvis pressed a button in a console beside the pintable. The library that filled the far wall rolled away to reveal a wide movie screen. Charlie turned his chair and stared at the pearling surface. The film, a Merton Park production, was *Sea Bird*. Shona Sage was cast as Gloria, the millionaire yacht-owner's sultry mistress. 'Earl's idea,' Jarvis Green said. 'When they couldn't get Jean Kent.'

'Earl?'

'St John. Ran Pinewood. Into the ground eventually. American.'

'Where do you line up, as a matter of interest, in the passport carriage department?'

'This is what I fell in love with,' Jarvis Green said.

Gloria sat on the foredeck and displayed cleavage that strained the buttonholes of her half-open shirt. When, after not very long, an accurate wave broke over the shirt it was rendered transparent.

Charlie said, 'Impressive buttons, I must say.'

Jarvis Green said, 'Aren't they? I bought the company that made that shirt.'

They watched a while longer, and Jarvis Green pressed a button and the library rolled back in over the screen.

'So . . . Rollo tells me that you're officially "the Honourable" Charles Marsden.'

'One of those English things you can't get easily out of.'

'Meaning you'll be a lord one day.'

'You may well beat me to the post at the present rate of striking.'

'But I shall never be an honourable.'

'There is the odd joker, even in today's rich and wonderful pack, that won't fit up any old body's Italian-style sleeve.'

'Who do you go to? For suits. I was going to ask you.'

'Woolies, don't I? Time I went and found a bus.'

'Seriously.'

Charlie said, 'Nothing wrong with Huntsman's that I know of. I can always warn them you're coming, if you want me to. But they take money with remarkably little fuss. Where's the nearest stop exactly, do you know?'

'Upstairs. You can't possibly go anywhere at this hour. Cater'll run you back into town in the a.m.'

'If he's going that way.'

'He will be. Before you go . . . Norton, Wilment . . .' Jarvis looked at Charlie's cheque and then he tore it in four pieces. 'I could do with some help in that particular department.'

'Then you shouldn't have done what you just did, should you? Quid pro quo isn't a game I like to play.'

'Allow me my pleasures,' Jarvis said. 'It's not as if I'm asking anything in return. I could always ring someone myself, but . . . if you can bear to take the credit . . .'

'For what exactly?'

'Landing your friends the fish that just might lay the golden eggs, if someone will kindly press button A. In the imminent global finance department. Nothing Bernie C-like about me, Charles. Check the record. Everyone wins, if they choose to play.'

'Give me thirty seconds and I'll put in a word. I can't promise how many letters it'll have.'

'Listen, by all means make out that, from where you sit, the whole thing looks a little risky. People of your chairman's generation and social standing always like what's safe to seem dangerous as well. But then who doesn't? I will, as the sort of people you don't mix with so often say, see you right, if all goes swimmingly.'

'I rather think I ought to write you another cheque, Jarvis.'

'Meaning you're going to or you're not going to?'

'Make it out to Gunga Din, shall I?'

They laughed together, in different registers.

Jarvis Green accompanied Charlie to the second floor in the closet-sized cedarwood lift. The corridor was lined with paintings, in antique and modern frames, some double-parked as if in storage.

'As you can see, I buy quite a lot of art.'

'So you do indeed. Time you sold some, possibly.'

A wedge of light was spilling from a half-open door towards the end of the corridor. A man, in butler's waist-coat and black trousers, and a young blonde maid, in proper cap and apron, were turning down the counter-pane on the large bed, quite as if four in the morning was the usual time for such an activity. The man took a step into the bathroom to confirm that everything was as it should be.

'Thank you, Morton. And you, Inge.' The two servants went out. 'All right if I call you Charlie?'

'My dear fellow, it feels as though you already had!'

'But is it all right? So . . . if there's anything you want . . .'

'I should ask your wife for it, is that the situation?'

Jarvis frowned, as if that was a symptom of being amused, looked round the room, wiped his glasses on a tissue extracted from the floral container on the bureau and wished Charlie goodnight.

'And you,' Charlie said.

'Do call me Jarvis. You haven't called me anything so far. Yes, I have noticed.'

'I was waiting for per,' Charlie said.

The room was decorated with paintings by various hands. Charlie glanced at them and went to the short wall adjacent to the draped windows. The small oil painting that hung there, in a white wooden box frame, showed one bottle, with a narrow neck, of fumed glass inside a clear one of the same form. The title, spelt out on a metal strip, was *The Fighting Temeraire*. Charlie took the picture from the wall and turned it over. The raw canvas was initialled K.L.

He was aware of a tactful sound. The blonde maid was standing inside the door, which clicked behind her.

She had removed the cap and apron and let down her hair. 'Mr Green said to ask if there was anything else I could do for you, sir.'

'Tell me, what's your name?'

'Inge.'

'No, Inge, nothing; thank you. But then again: Mrs Green, does she live in this house?'

'Mrs Green has her own . . . staff,' the girl said. 'There's a bell if you need anything at any time, sir.'

He looked at the girl and she looked back. He smiled. She did not.

Almost behind the curtain on the other side of the window was another small canvas: a South London street scene with a brightly lit sandwich bar, its wide steamed window slightly off-centre. The title, printed all in capitals on a metal strip, was *Desert Warfare*.

28

Anya was in the living-room of the Albert Court flat looking at herself in a round gilt mirror. She was sporting a new set of black-and-red underwear. On the double canapé were two coloured cardboard boxes with tissue paper in them. Charlie was at his elongated ease in one of the flanking armchairs.

Anya said, 'You are very, very naughty.' Her quite abundant, now black, hair was contained under a decorative bandanna.

'I can't leave it all to you,' Charlie said.

'To stay away so long.'

'*Noblesse* strikes again, I'm sorry to say.'

'Your father. Did he . . . mean a lot to you?'

'Nothing neither way in that department. Civilities were observed, eulogy delivered, cousins saluted.'

'But still.'

'Indeed. Mortality's the only form of buggery we still don't choose to talk about all that much. I do also have this job. For some reason I'm rather in demand these days.'

'This man.' Anya stepped away from the mirror and went to where she had left her clothes.

'Man?'

'You poke with.' She bent to sleeve herself in her black dress.

'Oh, Jarvis, you mean? Why are you putting that on?'

'I was hoping you'd ask, dear!'

'Play poker with. All in the line of duty, rather. If you've got nothing you need to do, I'd like to kiss your lily-white back all the way down to those dark hairs just before . . . the great divide. And then not necessarily stop.'

Anya said, 'I don't ever want us to stop, Charlie dear, ever.'

29

29. *Scene of the Crime.* Whitewash on canvas. 40 x 32.
Not for sale.

30

Charlie leaned to peer through the soundproof glass porthole of Norton, Wilment's Partners' Room. Oleg Eriksen was indicating to young Holbrooke to fill Jarvis Green's glass and not to forget to refill Fred Kirby's. The felted door sighed as Charlie twisted the recessed golden knob and pressed it open on its broad leather hinges. The carpet was deep blue. The large room was panelled and, so visitors were promised, soundproof.

'Morning!'

'There you are, Charles,' Otho Augsberg said. 'We were only just not talking about you!'

Otho had been at the same school as Charlie. His grandfather, who had died while attacking Verdun in 1916, had been to an English public school near Godalming, Surrey. He had his name, Prince Franz-Alexandre zu Augsberg, inscribed on the roll of honour in Memorial Cloister for Old Boys who Died for Their Country in the Great War but in a distinct column.

'Good lordship,' Jarvis said, 'if it isn't Charlesworth!'

Oleg said, 'The Tio Pepe's chilled, Charles, if that's any sort of use to you. You know Fred Kirby, doyen of the Daily Dozen.'

'Sorry to hear about your father, Marsden.'

'Thank you.'

Jarvis Green said, 'Presumably this means that all your friends are now going to have to call you "my lord".'

'Not all of them, Jarvis. Only you.'

Oleg smiled, quite as if Charlie's remark was a compliment, and took Jarvis by the forearm and led him to the window seat. Fred Kirby limped a pace or two in the other direction. 'Have I missed something, old boy?'

Charlie said, 'Has your right hand lost its cunning, Fred? I doubt it.'

'I rather thought Master Green was the guest of honour.'

'Why are thieves said to be thick, Fred? Are they, in your experience?'

'Only the thick ones, old boy; i.e. the ones that get caught. Why?'

A side door opened and a man in black tail coat and striped trousers stood into the room. 'Luncheon is served, gentlemen.'

'Off we should probably go then,' Eriksen said, 'before the Sancerre gets cold.'

Jarvis said, 'Isn't it meant to be cold, Sancerre?'

'The Chairman will have his little joke,' Charlie said, 'the kind it's rude to laugh at.'

Jarvis put his arm around Charlie's shoulder, but Charlie insisted that the guest of honour go first through the heavy doorway.

The Chairman's dining-room had genuine Sheraton chairs around an oval mahogany table. An extra panel in the middle displayed the founder Aubrey Wilment's serpentine William and Mary silver candlesticks. The table was laid in such a way that no one had to be seen to preside. Oleg Eriksen went to the right-hand off-centre chair at the top of the table.

Charlie chose to sit at a modest distance from the Chairman, no one on his left, Fred Kirby on his right. They were served with devilled eggs yolked with caviare; crown of lamb, not unduly rare, with glazed parsnips, purée of Brussels sprouts with plenty of butter and pepper, sauté potatoes in quite thick, crisp slices. Apart from redcurrant conserve, there was always mango chutney, in a tubby oriental jar, on the table at Norton, Wilment lunches, regardless of the menu. It was known as Mr Roy's special. Roy St John Norton died in 1887. They drank three bottles of Château Cheval Blanc 1955.

After the cheese, fruit and liqueurs a choice of vertical cigars in cedarwood humidors was wheeled round on a brown trolley. The Chairman rolled his Antonio y Cleopatra (tact required the same choice, right or wrong, that he had just observed Fred Kirby to make) under his nose and said, 'I'm prepared to bet that you're in little or less doubt why we're here, some of us. Fred, as this establishment's favourite City Editor . . .'

'I presumed that I was the only one who was actually in his office, old boy, when your convenor made the call.'

'Modesty becomes you, Frederick, but fails you on this occasion. We thought you should be privileged to be the first to hear, officially at least, of our plans to set up the Norton-Green Commodity Fund. Otho here has all the dull details in terms of facts, figures and attendant fudge. Our springboard idea being that Norton-Green Opportunities, as we're calling it –'

Jarvis said, 'Point of order, Mr Chairman, literally! I have Green-Norton, Oleg, on my hymn-sheet.' Jarvis winked at Charlie, who agreed to be amused.

'Much it matters,' Oleg Eriksen said.

'Only reason I raised it, Oleg, obviously.'

'Is he right at all?'

Otho checked his copy of the release and substituted it for the one in front of the Chairman. 'I think you'll find that the latest version does say –'

'If I do, no doubt I shall.' He chose to glare at young Holbrooke, quite as if the mistake, if there was one, had something to do with him. 'What's of capital importance is that this is yet another very happy day, in the onwards and upwards department, for Norton, Wilment and, we have to hope, for those whom we . . . welcome aboard.'

Jarvis Green sat straighter but did not stand up. 'It's an honour and a pleasure', he said, 'for Jarvis Green Associates to become equal partners with what I can only describe as a pillar of the City of London, founded 1779.'

'Hear, hear!' Charlie chose not to look at Fred Kirby.

Jarvis said, 'We look forward to an exciting and profitable – profit before excitement, if possible! – association between the tried and trusted on the one hand and, of course, on the other, Norton, Wilment!' In lieu of laughter Otho tapped three or four times on the table with the flat of the fingers on his right hand. Young Holbrooke did so just the once and then looked down under the table, as if he were counting his feet. 'I should like to add a special word of thanks to . . . his lordship here for introducing me to the *crème de la crème* . . . and to Frederick Kirby, of course.'

Fred Kirby contrived both to laugh in a sporting way and to watch Charlie Marsden with unwavering interest.

As they stood about after lunch, Fred said, 'I'll scan the bumf and try and concoct something tasty for Saturday's issue. With any luck, what's said there lasts at least the weekend before it gets fished and chipped.'

'If you need any clarification,' the Chairman said, 'Otho's always at the receipt of custom.'

Fred Kirby said, 'Feel like walking me to my bus at all, Charles?'

'My pleasure, guv.'

In the street, Fred limped a few yards towards where his driver was waiting by a parked blue Jaguar XK150. 'All right, Marsden C, what's your game exactly?'

'Real tennis, isn't it? Was, last time I looked.'

'In the crime *de la* crime department. What've you got on him, Master Jarvis? Who is anything but thick.'

'Fred, really! What kind of a mackerel do you take me for? Think I'd urge them into bed together if I thought Oleg might catch something crabby? Jarvis is the bright new generation in the shitty of London department. Comes up roses more often than you can count. Said so yourself, if I remember rightly when he dismantled Schneerson, Gilmour and sold off the pieces for ten times the number anyone had ever thought of. I put it to Oleg that if we chose to get in at the ground floor, or possibly lower, Jarvis might prove to be the kind of Sesame we needed.'

'Ever met any of the associates of J. Green and Associates?'

'Men of straw, I suspect, if as substantial as that. Poker players are liable to be loners, and he is one. As I have proved to my not undue cost.'

'No one doubts he knows his onions from his sprahts.' Fred Kirby helped his stiff leg into the car. 'I suspect you're playing up and playing the game, old boy. If you're ever disposed to be somewhat less cousinly, you won't fail to give Freddie boy a bell, will you?'

'As if I would, Frederick, as if I would!'

Along London Wall, in front of Norton, Wilment, where the metallic green Corniche was double-parked, Jarvis Green was shaking hands with Otho. As Cater drove him past Charlie, Jarvis gave him a wave. Charlie rather wished he had not sold the Morgan.

31

The success of The Gunroom impelled Theo Plant's syndicate of backers to fund his new venture, The Golden Bowl. He sited it at the end of Ebury Street in order not to draw custom from his other establishment near Chelsea Green. The walls were adorned with Victoriana. Gilt-framed cases held high-buttoned boots, riding crops, whalebone corsets and bloomers. Over the bar a large frame contained a full pack of *cartes de visite*. Most were of famous persons in polite postures, some signed; a few were of naked women and handsome youths of the unashamed, dangling brigade as photographed, in sepia, in Taormina by Wilhelm von Gloeden.

The wall adjacent to the kitchen door was filled with gilt mirrors of varying sizes, some aged with grey-black discoloration. The waitresses, in silent black slippers, were dressed in black bombazine with white lace aprons and starched coronets. The entranceway had a brass hoop over the top from which a heavy purple velvet curtain was suspended on thick brass rings. The floor was covered with a montage of Victorian carpets, some in quite small segments, tightly stitched to avoid bumps or actionable trips.

"Ot grapefruit!' Anya said. 'And two of zem! Your friend is very clever, dear, and very naughty with the cherry. Such a witty anniversary you are giving me, my darlingk!'

'My very dear Anyushka . . .'

'Suddenly you are writing me a letter, I sink. Is it one that I want to get, I 'ope?'

'So I trust – and hope.' Charlie had taken Anya's hands in both of his and was leaning across the round table. The velvet curtain rattled heavily as it was drawn aside. Katya Lowell was wearing high brown boots, a new, slim suede coat, with dark brown frogging across the breast, lighter fur at the throat and wrists. She removed her Cossack-style suede and fur hat and shook her hair, which budged hardly at all.

Jarvis Green entered doing covert things to his left eye. When he looked up, Charlie could see that he had dispensed with businesslike spectacles and, as he looked down again, and blinked, that he was having trouble with one of his contact lenses. He was wearing a grey suit of recognizable cut. As Katya waited, she was framed in several of the battery of mirrors. It seemed that, while Jarvis Green ducked to correct his vision, she was alone with Charlie. Anya heard him breathing and was not deceived. 'What's 'appened, dear?'

Theo Plant, in grey frock coat and butcher's apron and a knitted grey cap, was crossing towards them. He kissed Anya's hand and stretched the spare one towards Charlie, who failed to take it.

Katya was walking towards a tight alcove which the head waiter had indicated. Jarvis caught the *maître d*'s sleeve and pulled him towards the instalment of bank notes which he pressed into his hand. After a few words, 'Of course, Mr Green' the last, Jarvis was shown to a more ample alcove with room for four people to dine.

Katya had not noticed Jarvis's change of direction until she turned to see him on the other side of the room. He gestured to her, quite severely. She stood there. He gestured again. And then she went and joined him. He held her chair for her as she sat down. Charlie's mouth was slightly open as he breathed and breathed again, with tight fists. Theo had a hand on his shoulder. 'You're my guests, both of you. So . . .'

'You are so, so kind, dear. I love gestures.' Anya seemed to be speaking to the air, as if she feared looking again at Charlie.

'*Bonne continuation.*'

Anya said, 'You were about to say somesing, but I sink . . . I sink . . . somesing 'as 'appened. Tell me I am wrong.'

Charlie said, 'Dearest Anya . . .'

'I am right.'

'Dearest Anya, you've given me the most wonderful months of my life so far and I shall never forget them or you.'

'Too right.' She pushed away the grapefruit. 'I am finished now.'

Charlie said, 'Long ago we made a pact.'

'No, zat is not what we did.'

'Yes, we did.' He was unclenching his fists. 'That we would be . . . *honest.*' The pronounced aitch was enough for black tears to pop and spill on to Anya high cheeks. 'And never lie.'

'Zis is never what you were going to say to me when we sat down.'

'It's what has to be said now. To the effect that if either of us ever fell truly in love . . .'

'Who is she, Carlos? It is a *she*, isn't it?'

Charlie bit his top lip and looked away. Katya's bare arm and long hand, stretched on the top of a red plush banquette, were as much as they could see of her.

Anya said, 'That is the woman?'

'That is the woman.'

'And I thought we came 'ere to celebrate. You said you brought me 'ere to celebrate. You trickled me. You brought me to be . . . to be defeated.'

'I had no idea that she was coming here and no intention whatsoever of saying anything about her. She was not in my mind for a moment. Defeat doesn't come into it.'

'But you do . . . know her.'

'I have never so much as exchanged a single word with her.'

'You swear?'

'I swear.'

Anya looked at Katya's arm and then at Charlie. 'In zat case . . . I understand. Zat I 'ave no 'ope.' He leaned and kissed her. She shook her head. 'Whatsoever. Since when have you . . . ?'

'I first *saw* her, oh, months ago now.'

'And that's when it started.'

'My . . . interest, yes. In her work, mostly. Until tonight.'

'The man she is wiz. You know him.'

'Rather better than I know her. Much, in fact.'

'That has somesing to do with it.'

'I don't think so.'

'I am sure so.'

'Who knows for certain why triggers get pulled? I didn't even know she knew him.'

'He is not a good person.'

'I've always rather enjoyed that about him.'

'His eyes. Steely. Like loaded guns. I've known such men. Not nice when they go off.'

The waiter came and took away the grapefruit plates.

Anya said, 'Charlie, will you now please take me home, please? Now.'

Charlie looked across at Theo and conveyed, with a twist of the fingers close to his right eye, that something had happened with Anya that he was powerless to override. Theo understood.

They sat in silence as the taxi bore them to Prince Consort Road. Charlie got out first, helped Anya down, as if she were now much older, and walked her to the doorway of 9–16. The taxi's meter ticked behind them.

'Come up wiz me, Carlos. One more time. *Une fois pour toutes*, yes?'

'I can't toot tonight, my little Anyushka. *Rien ne va plus.* You know zis. Delightful as I well know it would be, I simply can't.'

'Love!' she said. 'We stay friends, yes?'

'Through sick and sin,' he said. 'We will never be

anything else. If you need me, you call me, without hesitation. But if I don't go now, we couldn't be, could we, friends?'

'You would 'ave to be cruel to me. And you could never be cruel, poor Charlie, could you? That is your misfortune; and mine maybe. So . . . I wish you luck with her, dear. I did teach you somesing, yes?'

'You taught me everysing.' He took her in his arms and kissed her eyes. 'And I shall never, never forget it, yes?'

'When you get 'er, you keep 'er.'

'When I get her, I marry her, my darling. That's . . .'

'No, no, I am not crying. I am not crying one little bit. You will be careful, Carlo, won't you, dear?'

He smiled, as if he would be, and walked back to his taxi.

32

THE UP AND THE COMING
By Frederick Kirby, City Editor

That no-nonsense, bold-school-tie high-flyer Jarvis 'Trust Me' Green promised me, over a modest three-wine, two-cigar (one for your top pocket) snack at that bank of venerable banks Norton, Wilment, that his and their new joint Commodity Fund is the most democratic ever devised by a duet of tycoons, ancient and modern, for the benefit of the likes of you and – forgive the intrusion – me. What but philanthropy on the march could lead Oleg Eriksen to team up with ex-knocker on doors turned asset-stripper extraordinaire J. Green and offer us all access to untold millions or a fraction of the same?

Mr Safe Pair of Hands, alias Norton, Wilment Chairman Oleg Erisken, assures me that he will do all he can to protect the small investor (minimum ante £2,000) against any kind of what he did not call smart-alecry on the part of his go-getting new-broom-mate. It just might happen that Jarvis's Jolly Roger will soon have its own pole atop 3 London Wall, where N.M.'s banner so proudly flies. Watch that space! And remember where you read it first.

Charlie, alone at Saturday breakfast in Beaufort Street, tore the City page of the *Daily Crusader* out of the paper, folded it carefully in four and pressed it down in the toaster.

33

10. *Some Talk of Alexander.* A strong not very young man, naked to the waist, in an athletic club changing-room, is fitting a bra to his hirsute breast. A fencing mask is on the chair next to him. He is wearing white athletic trousers and boots appropriate to fencing. Behind him, hanging in one of a set of metal lockers, is a lion's skin and a lady's veiled hat. Oil on board. 42 x 38.

34

'But why now, my dear chap, just when you've done us so signally proud with your endeavours? Your bonus, should Christmas come, threatens to double your usual screw.'

'Make no mistake, Chairman. I've enjoyed it all enormously.'

'That I can forgive,' Oleg said. 'Up to a point. But . . . are you thinking of going elsewhere? Has something happened that I ought to be aware of?'

'Almost certainly. But nothing that I should care to disclose, even if I were sure what it was. Let's just say . . . I've got these acres to concern myself with. There seems to be quite a chunk of Wiltshire that my papa parcelled in some kind of a Channel Island trust along with Marsden Old Place. And also I need to dispose of his dank Irish pile, if I can find anyone who fancies somewhere with moss on the walls; inside them, I mean.'

'And that's the truth, is it?'

'Enough as need concern us here.'

The change of tone was enough to make the Chairman stand up. Charlie had the courtesy to get to his feet quickly enough to seem to have done so first. They had been sitting in two leather armchairs across from Oleg's big desk in the window. 'I shan't forget what you did, however, in bringing Jarvis to us.'

'I earnestly hope you won't have to, Chairman.'

'Oleg. Oleg, please, from now on. The fund's almost twice its offer price thus far. Early days are often the best, but so far so bullish. You don't have any reason . . . ?'

'No rhyme and no reason. Long may it last.'

'Long enough for us to get out without a commotion, if needs be! Do stay in touch, Charles. Come and have lunch and remind us of the error of our ways. And good luck with . . . the acres.'

A week later, Charlie took Fred Kirby to lunch at Overton's in St James's. Kirby ordered whitebait and steak tartare; Charlie had the fresh asparagus and a grilled Dover sole. 'And a bottle of Château Cissac. The '53 ain't bad. Promises to clash handsomely with my fish.'

Fred Kirby said, 'Off the record, what've you got against him, old boy?'

'There *is* no record, that I know of. Rather why we're here. It occurred to me that you might know something I didn't.'

'Quite a lot, I imagine. And v.v., I suspect.'

'He does cheat at cards. Personal experience, as the footnotes say.'

'Got burned, did you?'

'Singed. Nothing that's going to leave a scar. He's not any kind of serious card-sharp these days, and he's certainly an excellent host. May well have been different back when.'

'Why should he still do it, given the size of the bunce in his back pocket among other less likely places?'

'It's a skill with him,' Charlie said, 'never a necessity, cheating. He may well like to keep his hand in, the way old Wally Robins used to put himself on to bowl to make sure he still had a tweak left in him. People fancy seeing if they can still serve up a googly one way and another.'

'Point there! It's even been known for the odd journalist to push a share he bought just before his paper went to press with the tip of the week.'

'You shock me, Fred. In the ordinary way of trade, he goes out of his way to be generous, does Jarvis. At the same time, he can't resist seeing what he can get away with. Which just might, in my unsubstantiated view, include murder. One more way of keeping his hand in, maybe.'

'Somebody you know?'

'Once saw; and didn't all that much care for. Master J's quite welcome to murder him, if that's what he did. But if it is, I'd be interested to know. And why.'

'What's your grudge suddenly?'

'Not sure. I quite like his company.'

'A spot of *cherchez la femme* going on at all?'

'Is Kirby also among the prophets?'

'Much it matters, but Fred can sometimes tell. And also not tell, as the agenda may have it. However small the potatoes, I have my master's p's and q's to attend to.'

'DSO, DSC you got in the war. Enviable, that. I looked you up.'

'You've got two legs, old boy,' Fred Kirby said. 'So that's that. Very good, this plonk.'

'Better a bad wine in a good year than a good wine in a bad one.'

'Is that what they say?'

'I've never heard them. True, though.'

Fred said, 'One thing you must know that I know: my lord and master wouldn't look kindly on Chummy falling too suddenly, too heavily, not so soon after we've rather encouraged the mutton-headed readership to put their nest-eggs in the cockatrice's whatsit.'

'How many of the mostly very dull people sitting in here munching have killed people, do you suppose, Fred?'

'Depends on whether you mean did they see what they were doing. I never did personally; which doesn't prevent me hoping that a few of our torpedoes went bubbling off to do something lethal. Not more than 5 per cent of people in the services ever saw the whites of anyone's eyes who wasn't on their own side. Who do you think he killed when?'

'Had killed, is likelier. And I don't mean in the war.'

'Now you're talking.'

'One Harry Groves, for instance.'

'Same one as his father had a greengrocer's shop in Kensal Rise? Tough little bastard, quite a scalp-collector, Master G, in the mustard-and-cress department from all I hear; one-time sidekick of George Dawson. Second and subsequent times, did it on his own. Same chap?'

'Could very well be.'

'Unlikely company for you to keep, old boy.'

'I only saw him but the once.'

'A lot of girls, nice and otherwise, have been known to say the same thing.'

'He was a Desert Rat, then SAS very probably. My

sources tell me that he may've been seconded to SOE. Bilingual, apparently; Belgian mother. One rarely wonders what people's mothers were called when in an unbroached state. After the war, if not a little sooner than that, he went into scrap. In the first instance, so I've been told, in France and Italy. A lot of metallic objects were going for a song, but you still needed to sing it properly, or improperly. My guess, wild but not woolly, is that he funded his later operations from a kitty donated by HMG, although not for the purpose to which he put it. Lots of sovs were going around in suitcases, and receipts were rarely given. Word is, he managed to repatriate some of the funds, most likely by boat to some remote cove. He then made quite a bundle in the UK metal market before the bottom fell out. Tough customer, by all accounts. Not an easy mark to put away in the normal way of trade.'

'You've been a bit diligent, old boy, haven't you, for a man of your cut?'

'I had some help in the where-to-dig department. He had some qualities, did Master Groves.'

'What happened to him exactly, do you know?'

'He was suffocated. After they'd done quite a few nasty things to him. No one was ever caught.'

'What interest might Master Jarvis G have in laying him to rest?'

'Two and two time.'

'Never need make four, if you've got access to a good accountant. Mine's called Cyril. Told me the other day that the woman he bumpsadaisies, Tuesdays and Fridays, will only do it when he's up behind her. That way she can ply her trade, read a mag and smoke at the same time. Master Jarvis. Two and two what? Any sex angle at all?'

'I'll have a word with the vicar,' Charlie said. 'More than likely. Inquiries continue.'

'If you come up with anything, three-in-a-bed style stuff, I can always alert one of my chums who works for the dirties and we can watch J. Green Esquire go down, if that's your wish, without ever upping our own arncher, as my ex-Free French first officer used to call it. Frog navy people often didn't like de Gaulle all that much. Funny thing about war: you can end up disliking your allies more than you hate the enemy.'

'I wouldn't want to make Jarvis any more popular than he is already.'

'It's just that what?'

'I'd like to have something solid on him, if only I knew what.'

'If ever you do, old boy, alert Uncle Fred first, won't you? Don't wash your spear or start war-crying without a preliminary quiet word.'

'My word on it,' Charlie said.

'And I'll report to you likewise.' Fred Kirby held out his hand. 'Gentleman's agreement.'

'Who's the other gentleman?'

'A flea in your ear, Master Marsden. There are things you ought possibly to resist, but I doubt you ever will.'

'My dear Fred . . .'

'Is that French possibly for have a big cigar?'

'I rather think it better be, don't you?'

35

Camilla and Marcus had bought a pair of cottages in Swan Walk facing the lichened brick wall of the Chelsea Physic Garden. When Charlie arrived, Camilla was bathing little Piers. He lay on his back, water almost over his face, and kicked until a drop went in his eye. He blinked but did not cry. Charlie explained to his sister what he would be more than passing grateful for, if she could arrange. 'Shouldn't be any trouble at all,' she said. 'Marcus'll fix it. He can fix anything as long it's not a fuse.'

'He does look very like hubs, Mill, doesn't he? In some ways.'

'I do like my teapot to have a proper spout on it, if that's what you mean.'

'If it could all seem to be something approaching a coincidence, preferably not along the beaten path, that would be ideal.'

'Marcus relishes a spot of double-dealing, you know that. He's told me about a ripe selection.'

'You're one of a kind, sis. I hope he knows that.'

'I shall make sure that I never ask him. If we do it at Potts, assuming Tufts and Vinny are game, how would that be?'

'My cup might well run over.'

'I'll order some spring sunshine. You do know something, dear brother, don't you? You don't have to worry, not about me and Marcus and anyone else.'

'I wouldn't dream of it.'

'In the sense that I do love him, whatever. And he me, ditto. So don't even feel there's anything you have to say to anyone about anything.'

'I don't know what you're talking about, Mill, but I do advise you to stop.'

Invitations were sent to a dozen people, none of whom had reason to suspect that he or she was the object of the exercise, for the second Saturday in May. There would be tennis and croquet and a lunch and a proper tea and, for those who cared to stay for it, kitchen supper.

At the sit-where-you-like lunch in the morning room, a buffet was laid under the Francis Sartorius painting of a hunter. Charlie found a perch close to Katya Lowell, but neither next to nor directly opposite her. He nodded with a gallant show of interest as Vinny told him, at length, about an accountant and his wife who had moved into the second biggest house in the village and had bought so much jam and so many pastries at the church bazaar that it had caused a good deal of ill feeling.

After coffee, Pierre-Henri Drot, the bilingual cultural attaché at the French Embassy, was paired at croquet with Camilla against Lavinia and Marcus. The tennis court had been mown, rolled and marked. Charlie sat on the wall of the wide Portland stone terrace and watched Jeremy Glover and the ample, surprisingly agile Peregrine Savage play Gavin Holbrooke and Ferdy Plant. They objected, quite fiercely, to each other's line-calls, young Gavin less often than the others.

Charlie was doing the Brigadier a favour by giving his Purdey 12-bore a much-needed rodding after two rather protracted attacks on the rooks and, although no one was supposed to know, a bout of Ritchie-Hooking of the insurgent squirrels, some of whom had squeezed into the apple store and seemed to thrive on the poison which had been set out for them.

Charlie was aware, without looking up, that Katya Lowell had emerged from the house. She unfolded a canvas stool and sat herself, with a box of watercolours and a leggy easel, a few yards further down the terrace from where Charlie was squinting through one of the barrels of the now gleaming Purdey. She had changed into a semi-military top, of khaki and green cotton, and Turkish-style cotton trousers tucked into soft leather boots.

Marcus could be heard saying, 'Nice shooting, Mama!'

Then Camilla, '*Elle est terrible, ma belle-mère, n'est-ce pas, Pierre-Henri?*'

'*C'était un vrai coup de Jarnac, ce qu'elle a* bloody well done to us, again.' Pierre-Henri had been to Westminster before he went to Sciences Po.

Katya Lowell had pinned a sheet of cartridge paper to the board that she had set on the easel. Through the half-open french doors someone was beginning to play Schumann on the piano, almost quite well.

'We have mutual friends, it seems.' Charlie was

checking the other barrel and seemed almost to be speaking to himself.

Katya's eyes were measuring the grey, sad-backed hunter cropping the two-acre field. 'You play cards,' she said.

'You paint,' Charlie said. 'And you also dine.'

'I saw you, I remember, at the Golden Bowl.'

'You remember,' Charlie said. 'I shall never forget.'

'You know Jarvis.'

'I know Jarvis.' He closed one eye and then the other as he did his final inspection before clicking home the barrels of the Purdey. He worked the chamois-leather rag on the stock and the triggers. 'And I love you.'

Katya washed her brush and smiled at something that was happening on the tennis court.

'I rather presume you know that. From lunch.'

'You never said a word to me at lunch.'

'I was very demonstrative with the cruet, I thought.'

There was the sound of a shot and then another in the distance. Inky rooks spilled up into the wide sky over to the left of them. The rejuvenated grey hunter cantered across the field, head plunging.

'Do you ride at all?'

'I did at one time,' she said.

'And liked it?'

'Yes, I did.'

'I'll bet you were good.'

'Fair. It takes time to be good. I didn't have it. So I stopped.'

'I used to ride quite often when I was in Ireland.

Visiting my late papa. I saw you first a longish time ago. At my friend Ferdy's. With a man called Groves.'

'Did you? Poor Harry.'

'You didn't love him, did you?'

'Love Harry?'

'None of my business. I realize that. You know what happened to him.'

'Of course.'

'Who do you think did it?'

She made a dark mark on the pinned paper in front of her, as if it were something that couldn't wait. 'No idea.'

'He was something of a hero at one time, so I was told.'

There was another shot. Rooks again scrawled black weals in the broad air. Charlie walked a pace or two towards where Katya Lowell was working.

'He evidently had enemies,' she said.

'Or funny friends.'

'Why are castles in chess called rooks?' Katya Lowell said. 'Do you know at all?'

Charlie said, 'At this moment I should like to have the answer to that question more than anything in the world.'

'Perhaps they're just two names for the same thing.'

'Like fire and water.'

She made a careful, seemingly random, green mark on her white paper.

Charlie said, 'I should like to marry you.'

'I understand.'

He was close enough to see her left hand as she rested it on the parapet of the terrace. There was a dull steel ring on one finger, like a single shackle. She was about to make another mark, but then she took the brush back towards her colours. She appeared in serene control of herself and what she was doing. He sensed, unless he only hoped, that his words had provoked some quiet commotion in her.

They heard another shot and then another; and were not surprised. She was looking at him steadily. It was enough to change his expression. He was at once wounded and, he liked to think, stronger.

'I'm serious,' he said.

'Do I doubt it?'

'I thought it was your work,' he said. 'I saw you at Ferdy's and I was curious about Harry Groves and about you, and I wanted to see some of your work. Own some of it, if possible. Latterly, one in particular.'

'So I hear.'

Whoever was playing the piano was now doing so with more confidence and volume.

'*Will There Be Anything Else?*'

She said, 'He'll never let you have it. If only because he knows you want it.'

'He told me it was his wife's.'

'I doubt if she's aware of it.'

'Is she actually still alive?'

'No reason why not. She keeps being reported to be doing things in various places.'

'She must be more than a bit older than he is.'

Katya Lowell said, 'He thought at the time she was quite an acquisition.' She made a mark on the paper pinned in front of her. 'He didn't know how far he was going to go.'

'And then that night at The Golden Bowl I realized that it wasn't your work I care about. It was you. It is you. It always will be.'

'You were with a woman.'

'Yes, I was. That I was about to . . . propose to.'

'You hurt her.'

'Last thing I wanted to do, but – yes – I did.'

'Was there a certain pleasure in it, all the same, did you find?'

'Not a scrap.'

'I'm afraid you may be a very nice man.'

Pierre-Henri could be heard to say, '*Ca, c'est joli, Camilla. Même très!*'

Charlie said, 'A love like mine for you can never be repeated or rescinded.'

Her smile cleared. 'I'm sorry.'

'I'll do anything you ask me to. Anything. If it helps. Or even if it doesn't. You have only to say the word.'

'I'll remember.' She was reloading her thinnest brush, the tip only.

'I can't believe that you're happy as you are.'

She made a mark without hesitation and smiled, not at him.

Charlie said, 'You didn't want him dead, did you? Harry Groves.'

'Far from it.'

'Is that why, possibly?'

The piano playing had stopped.

'Why what?'

'He is. Dead.'

The half-open french doors were opened further to make room for the Brigadier. 'Am I an impatient man? I am not an impatient man. I have gone through my entire pianoforte repertoire, twice, as you may have noticed, without anyone giving so much as an atom of thought to putting on the kettle. Is a man never to get his tea? Yet they still call it England.'

Charlie and Katya shared the reproach, which made it a favour.

'Who shall blame me,' the Brigadier said, in a reduced tone, 'if I now go down into the winter garden – as madam insists on calling it for reasons of her own fabrication – and display my main armament to the entire assembled company?'

Katya Lowell looked almost angry as Charlie's smile broadened at the sight of hers. He had tricked her, she seemed to imply, into an unwarranted moment of simultaneous humour.

'May I see you again?'

'I'm visible,' she said. 'Why should you not?'

Without haste, she loaded her paints into her box, folded her easel and took all her belongings, neatly, past the Brigadier and into the house. She passed into the shade, avoiding the Brigadier on one side and, on the other, a hollow elephant's foot containing four walking sticks, an antique alpenstock, two umbrellas and a riding crop.

'Didn't say the wrong thing, Marsden, at all, did I?'

'As if you could, Brigadier!'

'I wasn't meaning that *she* should put the kettle on.'

'I doubt very much that she took your words in that sense, Brigadier.'

'Interrupt something, did I?'

'Only something of the greatest possible importance.'

'That's all right then. Have you heard the latest?'

Charlie said, 'Not recently.'

'Some chap turned up to Dodo Brompton's shoot with an Alsatian. Expected it to be allowed to play retriever. It jumped out of the chap's overlarge motor and went for the other dogs like the legendary bat out of hell. Dodo told the fellow, "Fuck off out of here and take your bloody moggy with you." Can you imagine?'

'Easily,' Charlie said. 'Today being today.'

The croquet players were coming up the steps on to the terrace. Licky ran along the flagstones and went into the house, past the Brigadier, skittering on the parquet. 'Someone wants his tea and kiss-bits,' Lavinia said.

36

Charlie had driven down to Potts that morning alone in the new Alvis, of which he was less proud that he had imagined he would be. When he waved to a Morgan driver, forgetting that he was not driving his old darling, the other responded only with a frown.

After the captains and the kings had departed, as the Brigadier did not fail to put it, the family and Charlie ate scrambled eggs and smoked salmon in the Potts kitchen. The Brigadier would have preferred his bacon well done and said so. Camilla and Marcus had come down by train the night before and were now happy to have a lift back to town. Charlie, they recognized from his courtesy, his smiles to Lavinia and his silence, was not happy at all.

They were on the A40 before Camilla said, 'You should've driven her, instead of letting her get the train.'

'Her taxi was already there by the time I realized she was leaving. I offered to pay him off, but she said better she went on her own.'

'What had anyone done to make her go?'

Charlie glanced sideways at Camilla. 'No one had to do anything, sis. She elected to go; she went. Under cover of tea.'

'I hope you've made another date.'

'Dates are sticky things that tend to get imported from Turkey. I don't go bull on them.'

Charlie had put his foot down.

'What's the tearing hurry suddenly?' Camilla said. 'You used to rate speed.'

'That was before Piers.'

'Not to mention the somewhat imminent next in line.'

'I had noticed. I wasn't going to say anything,' Charlie said, 'in case it was wind or too much of Theo's latest food.'

Marcus said, 'Re the lady. More than one horse in the race, possibly? You'll be lucky to place.'

Charlie had driven several more miles before he said, 'Sorry about this, but as far as I'm concerned it's life and death.'

Camilla sighed in the renewed silence. 'Oh Charlesworth, it's only us, and you do know, don't you? *Nothing's* life and death. Not in the Home Counties. All Katya is is . . .'

The Alvis went into a sideslip. The tyres howled as the car yawed from side to side. 'What the fuck are you doing?' Marcus said. 'Camilla's pregnant, you total pronk.'

Charlie regained control, if he had ever lost it. 'All Katya is, as far as I'm concerned, sister, is everything in the whole wide, wearisome world.'

Marcus said, 'Leave her in the fridge where she belongs, is my advice.'

'You know nothing about her, my whoreson friend. Or anything else very much, however many points of access you frequent.'

'Fuck off, Charles, will you, any time soon?'

Camilla said, 'Oh please let's not do this, please.'

Charlie said, 'You weren't in any sort of danger, sis. You do know that, don't you? You saw me a few times in the old days at Brookwood with Papa's six-and-a-half litre Bentley.'

'I did. You nearly killed yourself.'

'And you can stop putting on the concerned parent face, Marco. It really isn't a good fit.'

'Friendships can be fragile, too,' Marcus said.

Camilla said, 'Oh, don't! Just don't! We only want you to be careful, Charl. You will be, won't you?'

Charlie nodded. 'Of course I won't.'

'Because I'd so hate to see you . . .'

'So very much should I; but if that's what happens, that's what will.'

Charlie looked at Marcus in the mirror. Marcus did not look at Charlie. They were almost at White City before he said, 'You'll never get her, Charlton, you do realize that, don't you?' Marcus's voice was pitched somewhere nearer concern than spite.

'Cool your porridge with it, Marco.'

'Facts of life.'

'I've always hated those. Ever since I caught my papa at it with an estate agent. Female, but all the same. Brenda.'

'Big-bum Brenda? You didn't.'

'Did I not? How shall we ever know?'

'Well, you must.'

'I once shot at a man when I was on patrol. In the Yemen. Neither peace nor war, supposedly. They were

128

said to be disturbers of the peace, mainly because they shot at us. I didn't know whether I hit him or not. Nor shall I ever.'

'He knew, presumably,' Marcus said.

'So did Papa, at the time, but now it's . . . believe it or not time!'

'I shall call you Ripley if you're not careful.'

'That's unlikely to make me so,' Charlie said. 'This looks like your stop.'

Marcus made rather a business of taking a small suitcase out of the Alvis's boot and checking that they had everything they had left with. Camilla had her door open. 'I do hate to go with you in this mood.'

'Nothing to worry about because nothing to be done.'

'Re Marco.'

'It's of no moment, sis, promise.'

'That's the thing; I'm afraid it'll be longer.'

'I gave you a horrid. I shouldn't've.'

'Can you forgive him, do you think?'

Charlie said, 'Have you seen the duelling pistols I got for Theo's new place?'

'Truth to tell, we rarely dine out these days. Is it nice?'

'Very. Not that I ate much. That was where I saw her with this man I know.'

'What about them? The duelling pistols.'

'I was thinking of Marcus and me. Don't think I won't miss him. But there's no turning back, none.'

'Ripley and Whittington on the same day, Charl? Overdoing it rather.'

37

Charlie arranged to meet Vince Baxter, if that was his name, at the Great Eastern Hotel. Baxter had told him that he lived near Chelmsford and was both poor and poorly. Charlie went to the bar to order the brandy and ginger ale Baxter had asked for and a pint of black velvet for himself. Baxter sat at a small corner table, facing the revolving doors. He was wearing a muffler and an army surplus overcoat, olive green with green plastic buttons. It was a warm day. A scuffed leather briefcase leaned against his chair. One of his legs was over it. When he coughed, which he did, at length, that leg was the only part of him that never budged.

Charlie took the drinks to the table and, while Baxter dosed his double brandy with ginger ale, remained standing. Charlie sat down only when he had taken a soft brown envelope from his inside pocket and put it under the Cinzano ashtray.

'Jarvis,' Charlie said.

Baxter felt the envelope but did not look inside. 'I first knew the subject when he was running a laundry. He was called Colin Grandage at the time. In the Netherlands Antilles.'

'Was he so? What sort of washing did he take in?'

'Sheets, didn't he? Balance sheets. Laundry without a laundry mark, that was his speciality. He didn't even have to be there to do the ironing.'

'Were the local authorities wise to him at all?'

'Very wise, in their own way: couldn't do enough for him. He brought the stuff in; they hung it out to dry. One hand washed the other. It was that kind of a laundry.' Baxter waited, as if for an enemy, in case he had to cough. 'In Guadeloupe he was Jean-Pierre Renault. French-Canadian. Passports for all seasons, Master G.'

'It was suggested to me that you might be able to find some material that would interest me.'

Baxter moved his leg and put the chapped briefcase on his lap. He had a selection of papers in his hand when a fit of coughing caused him first to flap and then to hold them out to Charlie, as if taking them would relieve the pain in his chest. 'Dates are on them,' he said, in a hollow whisper. 'Dates are on them.' He sat silent for a moment, apprehensive that the enemy was going to return. 'They indicate just how he . . . operated. And who for, in some cases.'

Charlie said, 'Anything I can get you?'

'I'm past doctors,' Baxter said. 'The undertaker's next.' He sat there again, waiting for the all clear. 'This set here . . . look at this . . . shows what kind of sums were involved and . . .' He waited again. 'They did these things more crudely fifteen, twenty years ago, because no one never thought the paperwork would come to light. Nothing was illegal, except where the money came from; and that didn't interest the Dutch, because that was why they were hanging on out there, wasn't it? Not to be interested. Of course it was.' He had said more than he had expected and now he was coughing; and coughing again.

'You were involved with him how exactly?'

'I don't do exactly, not even in my own head, not these days.'

Charlie scanned the typed pages with enough thoroughness to allow Baxter time to resume breathing, with mucous irregularity.

Charlie said, 'You had all this on him – why did you wait so long before . . . doing anything with it?'

'Do what, why? Use it and you've used it, haven't you? It was my insurance at the time. Why I'm still alive, unfortunately.'

'Time of what exactly?'

'That's a way we're not going to go, Mr Benson. I'm tempted to tell you, if only because you'd likely not believe it. Suffice it to say, I could run in those days and I could also jump. And I had a steady hand. Now, I don't imagine your friend would recognize me if he walked in here and saw me. You, on the other hand . . . I don't know what you've got in mind, but don't think he wouldn't do again what I know he did before because . . .'

'You helped him do it.'

'I'll say this: I saw it done, for him.'

'How is it that you're alive to tell the tale?'

'I take care. And your friend . . . he liked me. I knew what he was. I'd seen them in Germany, which I was in after the war. People do what they do and then they ask you what you're drinking. And you're not sorry. And then they want to know where the action is, nookie-wise, and it's your business to take them there. Seeing a man with a woman tells you quite a lot, if you choose to look.'

'How can I prove that Colin Grandage and . . . my friend are one and the same?'

Baxter nodded, as if Charlie had passed a test. He reached into the briefcase and brought out another packet of papers in a sealed transparent sleeve. 'Early work by Jarvis Green. He had to be somebody else, did Colin, because people can't give themselves two per mill and make out they had no choice in the matter. Third parties have their uses. Fingerprints are all over 'em, because I checked. Not a place to wear gloves in all that much, a yacht in the Caribbean. Which is what he sprang to, eventually. Quickly in, quicker out. That was his trademark.'

Charlie took another envelope out of his inside pocket and put it on the table, his hand on top of it. Baxter passed the sealed sleeve across to Charlie and Charlie released the envelope.

'You may think he's changed, Mr Benson. So does he, I shouldn't wonder. In my experience, people like him, whatever he calls himself, don't change and can't and wouldn't want to. Watch your back is all I'm saying. And don't forget your front either, come to that. He's done things make what I done seem like . . . Christmas. But sniff him. All you can smell is roses.'

Charlie stood up. Then he reached and took the briefcase from Baxter's lap and shook it over the chair he had just vacated. Nothing fell out.

'I don't blame you, Mr Benson, not caring to shake my hand. Neither do I, not all that much. Some of the places it's been, things it's done.'

38

3. *Punishment.* A table in a red button-seated alcove in a restaurant. A yellow rose, sleeved in a silver-paper scabbard, is laid, like a piece of cutlery, next to an octagonal black plate. An unused white napkin is steepled on the plate. One wine glass on the table is marked with lipstick; the other, otherwise clean, has a bite-sized segment where a mouth might have been. Two drops of blood are easing their way down from the break. A woman's black leather glove clasps the thin stem, as if it had just lowered the glass. Oil on canvas. 40 x 32.

39

Charlie, in new reading glasses from some people in Weymouth Street, spent unamused hours analysing the papers that Vince Baxter had passed to him. He typed up his notes, with two carbons, and deposited one set in his bank. Fred Kirby had given him access to the *Crusader*'s morgue, where he found jaundiced cuttings from Canadian and South African newspapers concerning the business and other activities of Colin Grandage and Jarvis Green. Charlie discovered that Jarvis had almost certainly had yet another *nom de guerre*: Leslie Sparks, a financier who operated out of Pretoria. In the late 1960s, the shares of Lubango Copper, of which 'the mysterious Mr Sparks' was Chairman, had rocketed, after the copper in its Angolan mines was said to be gold. Later, whatever metal was there proved to be neither gold nor copper. The share price fell sharply. The President of the country, who was left with a large number of Lubango's shares, ordered the arrest of the directors if any of them ever returned to the country. Leslie Sparks was never heard of again.

Charlie had written to Katya Lowell care of Rollo Farber. He said that he was going down to his family's acres in Wiltshire and had decided that the best way to get about on them was on horseback. Would she care to join him? There was a livery stables near by which could supply them with unexcitable mounts. He would come and collect her wherever she chose. There was no sort of hurry.

After three weeks of silence, he received a large stiff envelope by courier. It contained the sheet of paper on which she had been working when they were interrupted by the Brigadier. There were no more than a score of marks on the page. Their composition was enough to conjure up the image of the plunging grey hunter and the flurry of rooks in the silver sky.

On the other side of the page she proposed a date when, if it was all right with him, she would come to the address on his writing paper. He replied, via Rollo Farber, that the date and time that she had nominated was fine; he would be waiting outside in his car.

40

19. *Dangerous to Exceed the Stated Dose.* English wild flowers in a narrow-throated majolica vase, carefully rendered, on a mat of woven dyed grass. One or two of the same kind of flowers lie, withered, on the bureau, alongside a set of car keys and a half-unwrapped Crunchie Bar, with a bite out of it. Oil on canvas. 24 x 22.

41

She arrived on a bicycle with a pink frame, black taped handlebars. She was wearing blue jeans, black boots and a black leather top. Charlie watched as she lifted the bicycle on to the pavement and padlocked it to the railings in front of his address. She unslung her blue denim knapsack and then bent to unscrew the wing-nuts on the front wheel. By that time, Charlie was beside her. He took the detached wheel and put it, and her knapsack, in the boot of the Alvis. There was a bulging soft bag in there already and a wickerwork hamper.

'I used to have a Morgan, and like a fool I sold it. I think you might have preferred it.'

'Cars don't mean all that much to me,' she said.

'It's nice of you to take a day off. Did you finish something?'

'Do I ever? I'm always wishing I could get things back and do things to them. Quite . . . invasive things sometimes.'

'Art very long,' Charlie; 'life rarely so.'

'What've you been doing since we . . . ?'

'Digging,' Charlie said.

'Really? What for?'

'Victory, I suppose.'

'Yes? Over whom?'

'Never imagine that I'm not deadly serious, Katya Lowell, will you?'

Marsden Old Place had been unoccupied since the departure of Charlie's father to Connemara. Charlie and Katya Lowell rode in from the Binknoll stables along a tractor track which took them, like blatant spies, to the blind west side of the house. As they jogged round, they could see that only the wing in which Cheale, the bailiff, and his wife and daughters were living had clean windows. The early Georgian mansion endured dilapidation with ivied dignity. Charlie had not announced his coming, but Cheale appeared unsurprised.

'This is Miss Lowell. I thought she might like to see the place. How are things?'

'How do you do, miss? All right, my lord, by and large. The house could do with attention.'

'So I remember you saying when we were last in touch.'

'Old Berkeley isn't getting any younger.'

'But he's still able to do this and that, is he?'

'Not always on the same day, my lord.'

'Cheale taught me how to shoot. As far as not to close my eyes when I pressed the trigger. We're going to ride around the place a bit, Cheale, if that's all right with you.'

'Shall you be wanting accommodation, my lord?'

'Don't you worry about that. Good to see you. Molly well?'

'Thank you, sir.'

They rode along the wide gravel path at the back of the house. They could see over the brick wall of the unkempt rose garden.

'Only one thing really upsets me,' Charlie said, 'and that's not being able to show you the garden as it used to be. It's all I can do not to stop and do some weeding. I especially detest convolvulus. Perhaps because I almost like it. The nerve. And the twistiness.'

'Did you used to do a lot? Weeding?'

'God, no. We had people for weeding, and whiting, thinking of the tennis court. But look at the place now! Cheale and some gormless person from the village do their best, but . . . it used to be . . . something.'

'I like it like this.' They rode on into the swoop of pasture beyond the house. It sagged to a long shallow dip and then rose to a round, pillared, grey stone folly on the far crest. Charlie dismounted and helped Katya down. 'You really should live here, shouldn't you?' she said.

'Yours when you want it,' Charlie said.

'Charlie, you have to understand. That's why I wanted to see you.'

'You'd be surprised at how much I understand. It makes no difference whatsoever. If it would please you to have the place put right, it can be done. If not, it won't be.'

They had put their riding crops on the grey parapet in front of the ha-ha that circled the folly.

'You're a romantic,' Katya Lowell said.

'Of a kind,' he said.

'And you don't know there aren't any any more.'

'The kind that it never occurred to me could exist until I saw you, and your work. Titles . . .'

'No, I don't think they matter at all.'

'The ones you give your pictures.'

'Those I do. But not . . . all that much.'

'*Punishment*. Does it have a story at all?'

'It is one.'

'How you tell it is up to you. Is that right?'

'People sometimes say that.'

'And what do you sometimes reply if they do?'

'"Why not?"'

'It pleases you to be cryptic, someone told me.'

'The crypt doesn't have to have anything in it. The secret is to tell it in such a way that people . . . contribute an element that isn't there. I remember a story I read, German I think, about a perfect murder. Perfect murderer. He devised a poison with no innately harmful qualities whatever. Analysed in a laboratory, it was totally . . . anodyne. It required the collaboration of the victim, however involuntary, the admixture of the evil that was already in them, so the story went, for the dose to become lethal. It could never be proved, therefore, that the killer was responsible for the deaths of his victims. His poison did nothing but release what was already there in them.'

'*Ad*mixture is nice! So who is being punished in *Punishment*?'

Katya Lowell said, 'You, aren't you?'

'Might that have been your point?'

'If you say so,' she said.

'*Will There Be Anything Else?* That was the one I particularly wanted. But you know who bought it, don't you?'

'Why did you ask me to come out here today?'

'They have something in common,' Charlie said, 'and I thought you might tell me what it is. Now, in view of what you just said, I suspect it's because of me, not because of them, that they seem similar. They make me think about you, and when I do . . . I feel that you need to be . . . protected.'

'Your misfortune being that I don't. In fact, I wish . . . very much . . . not to be. Protected.'

'But you're part of the picture,' he said. 'So you have to say that, don't you?'

She said, 'We should go back.'

'That's not a direction open to us. Have you ever met . . . her? Yes, you do: know who I mean. His wife.'

'This is not having the effect you hope.'

'I can almost believe that there are people who can kill people and no one ever dares ask or even wonder what has become of them. People who can impose an . . . embargo on . . . curiosity so thorough that they can maintain the . . . is the word "eidolon"? . . . of somebody they have disposed of in such lifelike order that no questions are asked. And that – an element I may very well be contributing myself – is what encourages them to do such things.'

'Romance of that order has never interested me.'

Charlie said, 'What they have matters infinitely less to them than what they hope they may yet get away with. That way their motives leave no trace and their . . . actions need never be traced back to them.'

'That sounds more . . . elaborate than my . . . digestion can quite cope with.'

'Very nice of you,' he said. 'To take it badly. It almost gives me hope.'

'That's the worst of hell's conditions.'

'I know that, Katya Lowell. And I do realize that I can't have what I want merely because I want it. But I do believe something that you won't . . . entertain: that I can make you . . . what is there beyond happiness? Unafraid! I believe that I can make you unafraid.'

She looked at her little watch and picked up her riding crop. He caught her by the arm, gentle and arresting.

She said, 'And would I want that, do you suppose? Kill the fear, supposing it exists, and you kill the work.'

He said, 'You think nothing can be done. I think it can.'

'Enough,' she said.

'Enough is never enough; never was,' Charlie said. 'I ask only one thing, Katya Lowell, whoever you are or think you are: that you not confuse patience with weakness. He should know, whether you tell him or not, that this will never end; whatever you say, or don't. I should die, or kill, for you with equal . . . relief. You have only to say the word.'

'But I never shall.'

When they had returned their horses to the stables, Charlie said, 'We could always put up somewhere and do tomorrow what we never did today.'

'I'm promised,' she said.

'Then how about a snack? Theo ran one up for me in case.' He opened the back of the Alvis and took out the hamper.

Katya said, 'You're going to make things very hard for yourself, Charles Marsden.'

'You haven't read me right, Miss Lowell. You may do or not do as you wish, or even as you don't, but never make the mistake of thinking that you can . . . shake me off. My father used to have a rather too favourite joke, in which he'd say, "I have a fever, but I shall shake it off", and then he'd shudder like a wet dog. What I have, in regard to you, is not something that can be shaken off, by you or by me, however wet a dog I may seem. Now read on.'

They sat in the back seats of the Alvis and investigated Theo Plant's ingeniously packed lunch.

'His wife isn't dead. She's just . . . unpresentable. He treats her with great courtesy, always.'

'I'm not at all surprised,' Charlie said. 'I wonder why you agreed to come with me today.'

'Don't credit me, if credit is involved, with any solemn purpose. It seemed a nice idea to get out of London.'

'Does he know?'

Katya Lowell said, 'This isn't a line that's likely to go anywhere you'd like. I don't care to be . . . crowded.'

'Will you tell him where you spent the day and who with?'

'It depends on whether it comes up. I don't see him all that often. And he isn't unduly inquisitive.'

'But he is duly.'

'Do I understand you?'

'He asks you when he wants to, is that what you mean? Or is it that he asks you when you want him to?'

'I'm beginning to realize I probably made a mistake coming today.'

'No. You *want* to think that. In case he's listening. Or asks. You made no mistake at all. And that's what you wish was a mistake. If you tell him or if he knows, or finds out, what will he do to you? You wonder. Is *that* why you came, possibly?'

'You're being . . . inquisitive. I did not come for that.'

'I love you.'

'Or that. I truly do have to get back to town.'

They did not speak during the drive back to London. Charlie had said what he needed to say and had no wish to dissipate the effect with small talk. Her show of putting distance between them promised that they were closer. The beauty who sat next to him allowed what her words had denied: he had an effect on her. He was content with that, for the time being.

In Beaufort Street, he took her bicycle wheel from the boot and held it out to her. She applied it to the frame still shackled to his railings and tightened the wing-nuts. His failure to make a polite attempt to keep her with him made her somehow his servant. She looked at him, as she hoisted her knapsack on to her shoulders, with something close to disappointment.

Charlie said, 'Have you seen this new play that Benny Bligh is promising everyone is inextinguishably comic? *Mind the Gap.* We have to laugh or he'll never talk to any of us again.'

'I haven't seen anything.'

'What do you think of Benny B?'

'I don't. He's a dilettante.'

'Is that why you dropped him?'

'I'm not aware that I ever picked him up.'

'This imminent Friday,' Charlie said, 'I'll hook or crook some tickets. Will you come?'

She looked at him and then she wheeled her bicycle into the street and rode away into the busy evening. Charlie called out, 'Lights!'

She went a few yards further and then put one foot down. The red rear light on her bicycle flickered and came on. As she pedalled on, she raised a hand, as if in a reluctant, grateful vote.

42

8. *A Conceivable Solution.* A rural ditch, with a flowering hedge on one side. In the ditch are three cigarette ends, one (a filtertip) with lipstick on it, a sad scrap of newsprint, a soggy contraceptive and a dirty nailbrush. Oil on board. 32 x 24.

43

'You were too polite, dear. Zat was your mistake. You were not always so polite wiz me.' She looked at him kindly with those black eyes. 'You did not love me.'

'She sees him. That I know.'

'Poor Carlo. You are very young to be so old, dear.'

'These are excellent biscuits. Did you make them yourself?'

'Do you have to ask?'

'You're the only person I can talk to like this, Anyushka.'

'Yes? That hurts me very much.'

'I don't think so.'

'That you do nothing else.'

'Why him, do you suppose?'

'He's rich.'

'That can't be it.'

'Because you are rich, too?'

'Nothing like he is. Not ruthlessly. No, it's not money that attracts her; it's how he's made it. It's what he's done to people to get it, not its possession, that makes the difference.'

'She wants him to buy her,' Anya said, 'possibly.'

'She'll never let him. I'm sure of it.'

'Might that be where her pleasure comes in? And his . . .'

' . . . Frustration?'

'You like to think. Perhaps his satisfaction. You don't like to think. What he does to her makes her happy because . . . it doesn't.'

'You're being sage, Anyushka, and . . . continental. I'm not sure I want you to be. She sells her work and makes more money than she . . . needs. She rides a bicycle. She wears . . . clever clothes, but nothing . . . you see labels on in Bond Street. Money isn't to the point.'

'She is the label. That is what beauty does, dear. A woman like that . . .'

'There's no one like her.'

'There is only one thing for you to do, dear, and as quickly as you can.'

'Marry her.'

'Next time you are in bed wiz her, you must not be . . . so nice.'

Charlie said, 'I haven't been in bed with her. It's not funny. It's true.'

'It's as bad as zat,' Anya said.

'Worse. Better. Different.'

'Different is better; but better is sometimes worse.'

'Irrelevant then. Unimportant.'

'Zen why are we sitting here like zis? Why deny yourself what doesn't matter – and me?'

'I told you: I love her.'

'Per'aps she is 'appy as she is. Per'aps she doesn't like to bump her daisy. I like it. You know this. You like it too. Not everybody does. Let her go, Charlie. Settle for being happy wiz me and . . .'

'I wish I could.'

'Tell me what he does to her.'

'I don't know.'

'You guess. When a lover guesses, he wishes he had not; but that means he has. What? That games room of his you told me about, what does it tell you that you did not tell me about?'

'He doesn't play pool with her, I'm pretty sure of that. He buys her work. Perhaps that's what it's all about. Might it be that she's more . . . calculating than I care to . . . imagine?'

'What does she buy from him, dear, when he buys from her? Zat is my question. What does she give him the right to do that she wants and cannot have from someone she . . . ?'

'Finish your sentence, for Christ's sake. If you can.'

'I will say "likes".'

'Tell me,' Charlie said, 'how are sings wiz you? Have you found someone nice to do your ploughing?'

'Zere was one very pleasant, very muscular, exceptionally hairy person. From Bratislava, a bouncer, but 'e bounced off to work on a cruise liner where he gets bigger tips than here.'

'Dear Anya . . . '

'You are writing me one of your letters again I don't want, I sink.'

'You're the one person in the world that I can really trust.'

'That is so cruel, dear.'

He took a bite from his third biscuit and put it down and kissed her on one cheek.

'And 'ere, dear, also, you must!'

He kissed the other cheek. She stood in close to him; he touched her shoulder, like a fond memory. When she heard the soft click of the front door as he went out, she opened her eyes and smiled, as if it was a pleasure that she had been right. Then she took his unfinished biscuit and put the crescent that he had bitten from it to her lips.

Charlie was walking down Exhibition Road. He turned and saw a taxi, which slowed down as he looked at it. He did not raise his arm. He walked on to South Kensington and went into an estate agent a few yards down the Old Brompton Road and explained what he was looking for.

44

He spent the Thursday evening at Ferdy Plant's house. The director of the proposed film of *Whodunnit*, Bryan Price, had come, with his writer, Stanley Mason, to quiz them on what Oxford had been like in the late 1940s. Charlie was prompt with stories in which Ferdy played the part of the antic haymaker. Stanley Mason wanted to believe that Oxford undergraduates, especially those with smart affiliations, were more mutually endorsing than his own generation at Cambridge. Mellowed by doses of Taylor's 1960, Charlie remembered how the young Ferdy had contrived to be 'sconced' more regularly than could be explained by anything but an appetite for bibulous ostentation. Benny Bligh came, inevitably, into the solicited repertoire. He was the only man they had known who could charge a pound to come to his parties and hurt people's feelings by denying them an invitation to be taxed. On one occasion there had been an auction, so Ferdy claimed, for places by the door behind which a princess of the blood was having a tinkle.

Charlie was made older than he might have chosen by Price's thanks and the offer of a lift home. He elected to walk, almost smiling, down to the Fulham Road and then along Sidney Street. It had been a small holiday not to have thought for a moment about Katya Lowell. He paid little attention to the common smells on the stairs as he climbed to his front door and unlocked it, but when he had turned on the light he became alert, as if the *Whodunnit* mood had suddenly recurred. There was invisible cigarette smoke in the air. He checked the front door for signs of forced entry, found none and then went into his drawing-room. Nothing had been disturbed. The pictures were all there and hung as crooked as ever.

He walked round the corner to the drop-leaf table where he ate his solitary breakfasts. There was a bicycle wheel on the table, with recognizable wing-nuts on it. The wheel was bent and buckled, as if the tyre of a heavy lorry had driven over the middle of it. Charlie regarded himself in the round mirror by the kitchen door. He was glad to see that he looked singularly untroubled.

45

Benedict Bligh was standing in the foyer of the Royal Court Theatre in a proprietorial posture. As he had himself remarked, quite loudly, the success of Bill Orchard's *Mind the Gap* was the nearest to creation that a critic could come. Charlie was watching the door. He held a transparent box with a white orchid in it. Benedict Bligh had looked at his watch, twice, before Tamsin Fairfax came in.

'Cutting it fine rather, are you not, Ms T?'

'I probably shouldn't have come at all.'

'That would have been bold.'

'But I do want to see what all the fuss is about.'

'And so you shall, as soon as the curtain comes down and we've had a spot to eat.'

'Don't get the wrong idea about why I'm here, will you, Benedict?'

'What might the right idea be?'

The bell rang and a voice on the Tannoy announced that the curtain would rise in three minutes.

'That I succumbed . . .'

'Sounds juicy!'

'. . . To George's idea of a book about what he called "Now People". I'm not sure why. Independence, probably. I'm enjoying my freedom from deadlines.'

'Which leads me to understand perfectly why you have, as they say, come back to me.'

'If I was ever there. That profile I did of you back when was talked about quite a bit.'

'Oh, did it come out finally? We'd better go in. Master Humphrey has come out of his closet, I gather.'

'And straight down the drain,' Tamsin said. 'He looks terrible.'

'Curious', Benedict said, 'how rarely a man's true colours become him.'

Charlie was left alone in the foyer. He thought about the situation and found himself to be neither surprised nor fazed. He went to the door of the stalls and offered the orchid to the usherette, quite as if that had always been his intention. He sat next to the empty seat on his left and smiled at it once or twice when the audience laughed.

At the interval Charlie walked out into Sloane Square and along the King's Road to Beaufort Street. He sat down at the desk under the window and resumed his study of a fat collection of offprints from dated legal proceedings in the Bahamas. When the telephone rang, he did not hurry to answer.

'Hullo.'

'Charlie, it's Katya.'

'I know.'

'I just couldn't get there. So sorry. I hoped I might, but I couldn't. How was it? The play.'

'Hilarious.'

'And did you laugh?'

'You're right. Not once. Where are you, Katya?'

'I'm all right. It doesn't matter. I'm working. I like it at night.'

'When am I to see you?'

'Not now.'

'Because I must see you.'

'Try to understand.'

'Unfortunately I do. Unfortunately for him.'

'It's impossible. You must stop. Before something happens. Please accept that.'

'I want something to happen. In particular, I want you to get on your bike and come round.'

'I can't any more, and you know that precisely as well as I do.'

'Is he there with you? Because it makes no difference whatever, tell him. Or, yes, it does make a difference, because now, more than ever, I will never . . . mind the gap.'

'Goodbye, Charlie.'

'If you won't tell him, I certainly shall.'

'You don't know what he's capable of.'

'Better than any man alive, I suspect. If the dead could speak, it might be otherwise. Perhaps that's . . . no, I won't say that, but don't suppose that I can't imagine why you're . . . allowing this to happen. Why you can't resist it. I know very well and it makes no difference whatsoever. Once he knows that . . . it remains only for you to know it.'

He heard her draw breath and then the click of the telephone. He thought about it and smiled with one side of his mouth. Then he returned to his desk and worked at his dossier.

46

Tamsin said, 'What I find it difficult to imagine is the transition from, well, an occasion like this to . . . what you want to end up doing to people.'

'Do you?'

'If, as you say, you never have to bully anyone into . . . all right, submitting, how *do* you persuade them? I want to know the steps.'

'They are persuaded by themselves. Silence, for instance, is a great solvent. Like manners. Manners makyth woman too. The first thing is to allow her time to be just a little bit afraid. Once she has savoured a taste she has never known before . . . it's for her to decide whether she wants to go further. Not uncommonly she finds that she does. Just as, for all I know, dear Tamsin, you are wondering at this very moment whether to go or to come back to Ribbon Dance Mews with me and have nothing more to do with me yet again.'

'Is there ever a time when they can't say stop, your women?'

'I am conscious only of the sweet moment when they no longer wish to do so. Be comforted, if it comforts you; I have never forced anyone to . . . endure anything. My truest pleasure, the one that Ziggy never guessed, is to discover what women – the women I treasure, and I do – really, really want. Be assured of this, Miss T, I am not in the least concerned to know why. They bend to my will and, of course, my wont. That they do . . . *bend* is all the answer I seek.'

'The Bligh stammer once again disappears when there's a case to press.'

'You lean forward as you m-mock, I notice, thus affording me pleasure, and knowing you do. The female breasts, some studies c-claim, have become f-fetishized, notably in the US, as an unacknowledged displacement upwards of the female rump, the sweetest and most enticing flesh that a woman can offer for a man's pleasuring. It can last so much longer and has so much more delicious . . . refinements than routine rutting or pectoral pecking.'

'Have you said all this before? I suspect often.'

'You'd be surprised at how distinguished some of the audience have been. Are you coming with me to Ribbon Dance and help me play with my toys and all their pleasures prove? Now or never. Imagine how many times you will think about it, and wonder why you didn't, if you say no. The only power I have over you is your own curiosity, which takes several forms, does it not? How much will it hurt? And, more intriguing, how much shall I – you – wish it not to stop? Take your time, my succulent Ms T. You are the sole mistress of your f-fate. Is that a challenge you can resist? Imagine: you do the countdown. Nothing can be done unless you say so.'

47

20. *The Instruments of Torture.* A quill pen, ink, a telescope. Pen and ink on (torn) paper. 24 x 22.

48

Charlie walked back towards Beaufort Street along the
river from Flask Walk, where he had taken tea with
Camilla, Marcus, Piers and the recent Susanna. No
mention was made of Katya Lowell. The conversation
concerned Marsden Old Place. Camilla had no legal
interest in its future, but Charlie deemed it right that his
sister have a share in it. For the moment, he proposed to
leave Tom Cheale in charge; he had the respect of the
tenant farmers and contrived to sustain the property on
their revenues. The house itself, however, was not
Cheale's responsibility. Decisions would have to be made
if it was not to fall beyond repair. Oleg Eriksen had put
out feelers about forming a consortium to acquire some
of the land closest to Urchfont, which might be suitable
for upmarket development, if building permission could
be negotiated. Charlie sat adjacent to considerable
wealth but had no inclination to preen himself on it.

As he approached 15 Beaufort Street, two men in
dark coats and caps came down the steps.

'Good evening, my lord.'

'Cater! How are you?'

'And yourself, sir?'

'State your business Cater, why don't you?'

'I am commissioned to tell your lordship that there's
an event at the house. I was to indicate that you would
be a welcome participant.'

'Tell your master that, thanks all the same, I've subscribed to my full quota of charities for the season.' Charlie took out his key. The other man stepped between him and the door. 'Why is this gentleman with you?'

'In case I get lonely, my lord. Mr Green would greatly appreciate it if you would spare him a little time.'

Charlie looked at the other man. 'From the look of you, you didn't win all your fights. Reg, is it? More than likely.'

Cater said, 'It's the Merc, sir, over there, if you don't mind. No, the green one.'

'I shall come with you, Cater, because – believe it or not – I am more eager to hear what your master has to say, and more especially to withhold, than can make your muscular companion relevant to the case. In truth, whatever that commodity may be worth on today's market, his presence contributes nothing to the proceedings but bad breath and a hint of your master's anxiety. I'll tell you what would give this whole thing a touch of class: that's sending him home, with whatever is necessary tucked in his top pocket, if he springs to one, in a separate conveyance. Failing that, is there a glass partition in the second-class machine he's seen fit to have you drive?'

'Lord fucking Marsden.'

'And don't fucking forget it,' Charlie said. 'Reg.'

49

'Ten. Nine, eight, seven, six. Five. Four three two.'

50

7. *Mediterranean Diet.* An iceberg lettuce, with a deep
    cut in the top. Blood is running down to sauce a plate
    of *fusilli*. Oil on board. 32 x 20.

51

'One.'

52

Jarvis Green was sitting at the oval poker table, playing clock patience with a new deck of cards. He wore a dark-blue velvet dressing-gown over green silk pyjamas and stiff calligraphically monogrammed leather slippers.

Charlie said, 'Game over then?'

'There never was one.'

'Which accounts for the grateful absence of any reek of super-taxed armpit in this richly charmless annexe.'

Jarvis said, 'Nice to see you, Charlesworth.' The contact lenses enlarged the pale eyes. The hair looked thicker and darker. There was a glint of beard on the pallid jawline, no sign of it above the thin dry lips. He might just have returned from his holidays and had not had time to change back into his harder, businesslike self. 'I've missed you.'

'You should teach your chaps to show a little more respect for members of the Upper House.'

'I trust they weren't rude.' Jarvis was continuing to turn cards over in his patience game.

'Worse,' Charlie said. 'Informal.'

'I apologize.'

'You've got new eyes.'

'The next lot will be in the back of my head.'

'I thought you had those already.'

'That goes there and that goes there and that's that.

In this particular department.' He jumbled the cards. 'What can I offer you?'

'Jarvis, it's quite late and I've got some important sleeping to do. Why have I been . . . convened?

'You left the bank, I hear.'

'I heard the same,' Charlie said. 'The news wasn't exactly classified. And it's scarcely new.'

'But I didn't hear why. Why?'

'I no longer needed their tin, did I, or the company they kept?'

'And what are you doing now?' Jarvis pushed the used cards into a jagged heap and broke open a new pack.

Charlie said, 'Do you ever cheat at patience?'

'Well, I do like happy endings.' Jarvis put the clean pack on the table and tapped the top, inviting Charlie to cut the cards. When he failed to respond, Jarvis started to deal cards face up, without haste, one for him and one for Charlie. Charlie soon had a pair of queens and a jack. By the fourth card Jarvis had a pair of aces. The fifth gave Charlie a pair of jacks. Jarvis's last card was another ace.

'Demonstrating what exactly?'

'That you can never play against me and win, Charles. Even when you don't think you're playing.'

Charlie picked up the box and checked the name of the manufacturers. 'Bought them, too, have you? As it happens, Colin, I'm not playing.'

'I'll tell you what disappoints me. I thought we were friends.'

'That's not something one says. As soon as it has to

166

be said, it can't possibly be valid. Had a lot of friends in your life, have you, Col?'

'You've been seeing people.'

'A not uncommon consequence, unless one's very careful, of keeping one's eyes open.'

'You've changed your voice. That tells me something.'

'Might that be intentional, have you considered?'

'I preferred the old one. I've broken bigger men than you. And much more dangerous ones. I expect you've discovered that.'

'The problem can be what to do with the pieces, can't it, Leslie?'

Jarvis walked to one of his antique pin-tables. He turned on the lights and there were the gun-toting girls in Stetsons. He jerked up a silver ball and sent it cannoning among the flashing bollards. A tower of numbers built up on the panel next to the girls. Jarvis nudged the table to keep the ball on its buffeting career. When he did it again, more vigorously, to prevent the ball going down the drain, the panel flashed TILT! GAME OVER.

'Consider the possibility that everything you've discovered is what I'm delighted for you to know. On condition that you draw the right conclusions. And I do have a word of friendly advice, which I wanted to give you in person before things went any further.' Jarvis turned off the pin-table and walked to the back of the alcove. 'The art of business, I've discovered, partly thanks to you, includes the fact that the last place any of us wants to end up is the point of no return.'

'I'm quite fit these days,' Charlie said. 'Certainly fit enough to walk back to town.'

'Baxter.'

'One of your quondam friends. What about him?'

'What the hell is quondam and why do you use that sort of word?'

Charlie said, 'Nothing to worry about there. It only means "once upon a time", roughly.'

'But why use it?'

'Because I've been brought out here under duress, if that's a term I can use without exciting your disapproval, and I'd appreciate knowing why.'

'Well-known forger and blackmailer. Did time for both. Baxter. Show me a successful man, anywhere, who doesn't accumulate enemies. Enemies have to be earned. Friends can always be hired.'

'Did a famous name tell you that?'

'Quondam, I took a shine to you, Charlie. I did truly. From the first. Whatever you wanted of me, I was very happy that you should have it.'

'I've heard a lot about your wife, but I've yet to meet her. Seeing as I've come all this way, might that now be arranged?'

'Can you hear yourself? I can hear you. That voice, you think it's a weapon, I suspect. It's not. It's a liability. There isn't much of a quondam any longer in this country. Upper House! There's now and there's then. And never the twain shall meet. And if they do, now is going to trump then, every time.'

'I hear she uses a silver spoon. She wasn't born with

it, but she does use one, does she not? It's the only way she has, I hear, of getting out of where you . . . look after her.'

'Have you any idea of the risks you're running?'

'You're not going to turn out to be a silly ass, Jarvis, are you, after all this?'

'Or is that part of the excitement? It is for women. You know that. Even if you don't want to. Be careful of going too far.'

'Unlike some people', Charlie said, 'I might not be greatly mourned, but I should certainly be loudly missed. I do have friends and, since they derive absolutely no advantage from it, their affections, like my own, are remarkably durable. I should certainly leave a bigger hole than I actually fill in the normal way of things. And people will want to find out why it's there. My friends are friends, that's how quondam we all are, some of us.'

'Wind, Charlie Marsden, wind! Every word you say in that voice tells me how . . . how *passé* you – and your friends – really are.'

'Enter Monsieur Renault on quiet feet.'

'Never imagine Oleg is one of them, will you?'

'Oleg who are we talking about?' Charlie said.

'People who know it all can still be taught lessons.'

'Yes, well, you know the English: we never leave school if we can help it. On the other hand, we don't always warm to *arrivistes* who seek to jump a class; or play the beak. A famous name told you that. Stick it in your . . . book some time, I should.'

'No one could claim you didn't have your nerve.'

'And if they did, I'd certainly let them get away with it. There's nothing more foolish than a successful man who thinks that because he's made a packet he can wrap the whole world in string and brown paper and put it under his arm. People such as your good self can control many things and keep all sorts of folk in fee and fear, but you can never control everything. And something will always come along and, in the end, show you you can't. Every little Napoleon either continues on his way to Waterloo, via Moscow, or consents to make the best of a fairly good job and improves the street lighting on Elba.'

'Who the hell are you to come out here and patronize me?'

'If you're always going to cheat, old son, why bother to play?'

Jarvis said, 'You haven't got a serious bean you ever made on your own account. How could you possibly understand anything I do? I gather you like gardens.'

'Some gardens I do.'

'A garden's always under threat, isn't it, from weeds and such like? It's still worth looking after. Weeds will come, but a caring gardener knows how to . . . control them, doesn't he? If he chooses.'

'You cheat at cards, you fiddle the books, you . . . get rid of anyone who stands in your way. What the hell do you know or care about gardens?'

'They're not natural, are they, gardens? Weeds are. Convolvulus needs no help, makes no friends and has no enemies. It just . . . does what it does. Anything that gets the better of nature is a triumph of a kind. That's where gardens come in. Are you sure you don't want something? To own beauty is . . . what makes this worth while. Why else're you after that picture?'

'In that case,' Charlie said, 'why does your garden look like the municipal crematorium? Because it's you what's got it, possibly, although I should prefer to think otherwise. No, I do think otherwise. I didn't know it was yours when I first saw it. The pic, I mean.'

'There are more things in heaven and earth, aren't there? My garden's got some quite unusual things in it actually.'

Charlie said, 'In my book, crookery and horticulture have distinctly separate chapters.'

'When does it come out, your book?'

Charlie said, 'Why the hell am I here, Jarvis? Planning to pot me and then plant me in your garden, are you? Convolvulus! I take the ref.'

'You take money too seriously, Charlesworth. Gentlemen often do. That's why they never used to talk about it. Like buggery.'

'Did they not?'

'Suppose I took you on to the main board of Green, Wilment. You've seen where the shares are. Fifty grand a year basic, nix to do, car and a driver, and bonuses, of course, if all goes on going well.'

'Ah, the pinnacle of the temple! I was wondering how long it would take us to get up there. I've got a new motor, actually, and I do rate driving myself. One's less likely to go over a cliff that way. And it saves climbing into the same basket as all that dirty laundry you used to be – and, I don't doubt, still are – so adept at rendering whiter than white.'

'You know the trouble with the true-blue you, Lord M? You're more faded than you care to be told. You think you're playing the condescending toff; and so you are: playing is all you can ever do. Everything genuine in today's England is an imitation. Only the phoney is the genuine article.'

'And which door do you come in?'

'The same one you go out of, don't I? People like me are the genuine Elizabethans. We're the privateers and pirates who gave you your delusions of superiority. And not wanting us on board is what keeps you on the bridge after your bedtime. You just don't realize that with you in charge it's all sinking to the bottom. You found the world rigged in your favour, Charlie. Chance took care of you before they'd even cut the cord. Me, if I'd accepted things had to be as they were, I'd still be a bookie's runner in Earsldon, Essex.'

Charlie said, 'Yes, well, we can't all have your disadvantages, can we?'

'Contrary to the junk you think you've got on me, a great many people owe me a great deal, and quite a number of them are very, very grateful. You and your kind, they go down, who cares? Gamble it away, live on your fat, whatever you do, you do it only for you. Me, I go down, a lot of little ships go down with me.'

Charlie said, 'I don't spell shits with a p.'

'Schoolboy stuff is for schoolboys. Your chum Fred K's gorn and persuaded a lot of his nice readers to cast substantial lumps of bread, hard-earned in one or two cases, I daresay, on my waters. If the worst should come to the bloody awful – can happen, I know that – I have only to remove myself to foreign parts. Toss up between Lucerne, very dull, and the Costa Mucho, a bit noisy but not too bad in the upper reaches. Bruise me and you murder the munchniks. The only people who are ever properly punished are the innocent. I know that. You probably do, too. Now, if not before.' Jarvis blinked and touched his left eye. 'One takes it, up to a certain point, if things go south, and then . . . one leaves it. I already live, part of the time anyway, where you think you can send me. I like it down there. Midas sees very well in the dark.'

'Where the hell did you get that one from?'

'My son Jason. He's quite a scholar.'

'Then ask him where Minos is living these days. I'm not all that bothered about punishing anyone, Jarvis. I simply don't altogether fancy the enforced and prolonged company of a bucket of night-soil, however fancy its pyjamas.'

'I have some serious buddies who call me worse things than that, much, and then we crack a bottle and sing big swinging dick to the tune of ring-a-ring-a-roses. Where'd you get "enforced" from? Cater's sitting outside. He'll run you home whenever you say the word. Disappointed?'

Charlie said, 'Why am I here, Jarvis?'

'You like films, don't you?'

'Not over much,' Charlie said.

'Change of tone, do I detect?'

'I have to give you something, Jarvis.'

'Nothing I want, I don't suppose.'

'You're cleverer than one might guess from your overwritten slippers.'

Jarvis looked down at his feet. 'That's out of order, Charlie, that is, saying that, from where I stand. I've got one I'd particularly like you to see.'

'Sorry to say so, Jarvis, but Shona Sage was never top of my poppets.'

'That's all right. She isn't in this one.' Jarvis was turning down the lights. Now he rolled back the false library.

'I should appreciate talking to her, though. About that painting of hers. *Will There Be Anything Else?*'

'She's in Palm Springs at the moment. Did you not know? I thought you had your sources.'

'It's the picture I'm interested in, in truth.'

'Do you want a cigar? I can do better than Antonio y Cleopatra.'

'Why did Harry Groves die, Jarvis?'

'Later, if ever, Charlie. Meanwhile . . .'

53

'There we are.'

   'Bastard, aren't you?'

   'As widely advertised.'

   'You really are. I really ought to hate your guts.'

   'She said, because she didn't. D-doesn't.'

   'I'm married to a bugger, did you know that?'

   'Meaning you do choose them?'

   'Which doesn't worry me that much.'

   'Do I now guess why you told me?'

   'You knew.'

   'Not the same thing.'

   She said, 'That's not why.'

   'And you'll come again, won't you?'

   'Will I? Not because of what you did . . .'

   'Because of what you're hoping I'll do another time. We'll do. If you're good.'

   'Because – don't laugh – I love you, you bastard.'

54

28. *Bonsoir, Monsieur Courbet.* A rural crossroads. A shuttered cottage in the middle distance with a light on in the attic. Oil on board. 32 x 22.

55

The film appeared to have been shot in Super 8. It began with Morton coming out of a room on what seemed to be the topmost floor of Jarvis Green's house trailing a halter. It was attached to a barefoot woman wearing a towelling hood and a cape that reached almost to the floor. She resembled a cross between a medieval penitent and a visitor to a severely remedial spa.

Followed by the uneven camera, Morton led the woman along a corridor similar in scale to the one that Charlie had taken to reach Jarvis's playroom. Morton opened a door and showed the hooded woman into a room congruent, in its dimensions, with the one in which Jarvis was smoking a cigar and Charlie was not. The room in the film was thoroughly and distastefully furnished: velvet drapes, gilt mirrors and buttoned, tortuous Second Empire furniture. In the centre of the room was a plain metal single bed with a metal frame.

The barefoot woman walked across the varnished, seemingly unplaned floor. She trod carefully to the side of the bed. Morton indicated to her to kneel down. He then went to a walnut hutch that stood against the wall, under one of the gilt mirrors. He took a vase of white tulips from the top of the hutch and put it on the raw floor. He raised the lid of the hutch and took out a roll of tape, which he showed to the kneeling woman, as a wine-waiter might a bottle before pulling its cork. She nodded and held out her wrists.

On a cut, Morton was extracting a short-legged stool, upholstered like a lady's hassock in a village church, from under the bed. He eased it between the woman's knees so that one leg was on each side of it. Her wrists were attached to the iron frame on the far side of the uncomfortable mattress. More male nurse than gaoler, Morton taped the woman's ankles to the short legs of the hassock. He seemed solicitous of her approval. He stood back and looked at the whole arrangement, as an artist might at a floral arrangement.

Then he returned to the open hutch and came back with what was revealed to be a gag on black tapes. He administered the gag to her mouth and fastened it behind her head, over the hood, as if in some pre-agreed procedure. That done, he reached down and took the hem of the penitential garment, one hand on each side. It was then seen to consist of two long, wide, previously overlapping panels. The woman's white legs and buttocks became available.

Morton walked across, once more, to the hutch. The woman moved slightly as if to confirm that the panels of her robe fell symmetrically on each side. Morton came back with a thick, short stick of theatrical make-up. He took off the top and tried it on his wrist. Then he bent down and applied it carefully to the woman.

On a cut, Morton was at the head of the bed. He lifted the bulb of an electric bell from where it had been concealed behind the bolster and adjusted its position so that, without lifting her head, it was convenient to the woman's touch. Morton said, 'Ring when you're ready, madam.'

The camera stayed on the woman as the door of the room opened and was shut again. The woman did not move, but her breathing, through her nose, was just audible. The camera held on her.

As he smoked his rare cigar, Jarvis's eyes were on Charlie. After a minute or two of watching the woman kneeling there, Charlie said, 'I advise you to turn that bloody thing off, will you, please?'

Jarvis said, 'There's more to come you might . . . be inclined to see. When she does ring it eventually, the bell. What do you think the stripe is for? Have you guessed? Number nine, in case you're interested. The colour. Might be significant. *Target for Tonight*. Did you ever see it?'

'Turn it off, you total bastard.'

'"Please" is what nanny would've recommended, isn't it?'

'Please turn it off,' Charlie said.

'Better! Would you like to see the room where it was shot?'

'Why would I want to do that?'

'Because that's where she is, at this very moment. That's why the Corniche wasn't available.'

'Who was driving it, in that case?'

'The fancier the car, the easier to drive. I passed my test, first time, before I left Earlsdon. Driving and swimming, two things you can get good at anywhere. You ski. I don't. Skiiing had better come early or not at all in case you get snapped looking silly. So that's a bus I missed. I can skate, though.'

'Especially when the ice is thin enough.'

'You won't be all that proud of that, when you come to think about it.'

'Bluff.'

'Excuse me?'

'Is a suburban skill you didn't mention.'

'Call me and you lose, Charlie. You seem to forget: I always have the cards when I'm bluffing. What else are sleeves for?'

'What've you got on her, you sod?'

'She came to me. That's what you can't handle.'

'More bluff.'

'Be your age, Charlesworth. Or a little older, if you can work it.'

'I don't even believe that was her.'

'It didn't have to be. What is it they say: the fundamental things apply? The club is the club, isn't it, old boy, old boy?'

'I'd know if she were here.'

'That critic chap, Benedict Bligh. You must have been at Oxford with him.'

'What about him?'

'He had expensive tastes. Which makes him very . . . amenable.'

'Benedict's a ponce, always has been. Of the more entertaining kind. I'll give him that.'

'He'd sooner have a more practical kind of a bung, though, wouldn't he? Anyone who thinks ten grand is a lot of money is asking to be in someone else's power. I don't have anything much to do with him personally. I never go to the theatre unless it's an American musical. I hate intervals. Like you.'

'What are you getting at, for Christ's sake?'

'I sometimes give a g-grand or two to his favourite ch-charity. You know who that is. We exchange info.'

'You're hoping to put me off. You can't. I don't care what you did or do to her.'

'With her, Charlesworth. Is what bothers you.'

'You're a criminal, Jarvis, is what matters to me. Because that's a matter of facts and figures, and I have quite a lot of them, in a place you can never reach.'

'Of course you do. You think I don't give you credit? I give you all the credit in the world. I can afford it. And it doesn't matter to you in the least what I do or possibly have done. No, no, no; what matters to you is what you can't do a damn thing to change. It's me seeing to it that a beautiful naked woman gets what she ordered when she rings that bell. It's up to her, always, if she does or not. She called me and I went to get her. You're beginning to believe me. You're right to.'

'I'd opt for Lake Lucerne, if I were you. You could always learn to ski.'

'Too late and you know it. Does it occur to you at all

181

how exceptionally good-humoured I've been during all this?'

'True,' Charlie said. 'Not like you were with Harry Groves.'

'Harry Groves . . . overreached himself. He was his own biggest problem. Have you wondered why at all? I've been so . . . nice about everything?'

'Are you about to tell me that you really care about her?'

'Suppose it's you. That I really care about.'

'Oh, for God's sake.'

'I envy you. You know that. Not the title. Even when you deliberately wear the wrong things, it suits you. You're the one thing I can't have. But I'd still like to have a share of it. I had someone do some inquiries about you. Found out quite a bit. None of it . . . I was going to say none of it interested me. But all of it did, even though there was no way I could use it against you. You people, whatever you do, it always counts in your favour. That's why you're – in a manner of speaking – still alive, Charlie. So why don't we do the sensible thing?'

'Is this Colin speaking or Leslie or Jean-Pierre? Who is this? Anyone?'

'This is your friend Jarvis Green. Share her.'

'She's not a bloody fruit cake, and she's not a god-awful villa in Torremolinos.'

'She doesn't want you hurt,' Jarvis Green said. 'No more do I. Why not be . . . civilized?'

Charlie said, 'I don't know what you've got over her. I've tried to find out, but I still don't.'

'Nothing is all that difficult to find out. By which I mean . . .'

'She doesn't have any feelings about you whatsoever.'

'Why should she? It's nothing personal, Charlie. I've never called her. She always calls me. Since we first . . . got together. Thanks to BB. She comes and we talk and she has a glass of something, if she wants it, and then the time always comes when . . .'

Charlie flew at Jarvis Green almost before he knew he was doing it. Jarvis was stronger than Charlie expected. They fell against the table and then Jarvis was trying to get to the back of the annexe and Charlie was on him, just before Jarvis got to the rack with the pool cues on it. Too close for punches, they wrestled more than they punched. They seemed to conspire to make no loud noise. What was happening was between them. Jarvis must have had a way of summoning help. He took pleasure in not using it. They wrestled and took a breather and wrestled again. Jarvis was stronger than he looked, but Charlie was not surprised. He enjoyed putting him to the test, whoever he was. They fell against the pin-table and then across the pool table. Jarvis reached for a ball, gasped and smiled with pain when Charlie brought the white ball down on his fingers, but not as hard as he might have.

Jarvis moved with sudden determination, as if he had a gear left that Charlie had not suspected. He turned Charlie on to his back and Charlie had difficulty in holding him away. The fight was without humour now. That was the added fun. Charlie resisted as Jarvis

Green tried to force his face close to his. There was a wet smile on Jarvis's lips as he leaned on Charlie. He thought he was winning, and the mouth came closer. Charlie had room to swing the bolo and catch Jarvis under the seventh rib. The pain made Jarvis look happy.

56

16. *There Goes the Bell.* A small girl of five or six, on her knees, head down to look in at the ground floor, is playing with an open-fronted doll's house set at an angle to the frame. She looks serene. Flames are coming out of the side of the doll's house the girl cannot see. Oil on board. 38 x 24.

57

Charlie staggered out of the front door of Villa Verde and lurched across the gravel, past the cars. The front door was open behind him. He heard the sound of the bell ringing yet again. Heaving night air into his lungs, he blundered through thorny roses and on towards the electronically controlled gates. No one followed. No one was there. The gates opened before him, and he walked, more calmly now, into the night. The threat of morning streaked the low sky.

He relished the unshared air. He walked and walked into a suburban village street with a parade of sorry shops. There was a caff where steamy men in donkey jackets were drinking tea. Then he was in another tree-lined road with houses on both sides. He stretched as if he expected it to hurt and found that it did not. Something made him smile.

The green Corniche came up behind him without haste. The fumed window made it seem that the car was propelling itself. Charlie paid no attention. The car slowed down, and the passenger window slid down. A bundle, wrapped in newspaper, was thrown just ahead of where Charlie was walking.

The car drove on, neither slowly nor quickly. Charlie waited for a minute, to allow the Corniche to disappear, and then he bent down and opened the package. It contained a head of iceberg lettuce with a dressing of blood.

58

15. *Pastoral.* A shorn lamb enclosed in a stainless-steel pen. A benign-looking man in white overalls and a rubber apron is leaning on the top of the pen. Oil on canvas. 22 x 18.

59

Camilla said, 'That staircase of yours gets longer and longer.'

'Good for you, Mill. Get you back in shape.'

'Two down and none to go,' she said. 'That's quite enough of that. Not that I wouldn't have them and all that.'

'Marcus behaving?'

'He is rather. Should I be worrying?'

Charlie was putting papers into a zippered leather satchel. 'I hope this isn't too heavy, but here's the thing: anything happens to me, these go straight to Fred Kirby. There's another set at the bank, but that's strictly last-resort material.'

'Whatever's going to happen to you?'

'Road accident, bullet in the head, mysterious disappearance off the face of the earth, mundane things of that order.'

'Rubbish. All right, melodramatic. Aren't you being?'

'Careful is what I'm being. As nanny –'

'Didn't she, though? There are other women, Charl, if she's what it's all about, Lowell, K. Thousands, who'd suit you down to the ground. I know three. Two. One possibly.'

'I've never met one and I never shall. And I don't want to be suited down to the ground. Hence . . .'

'Oh Char! This isn't . . . you. I mean, why would any-one seriously want to kill you?'

'Milly dear, take these and go back to being happy with what you've got. Love is love. It doesn't leave room for conversation, not even with you, sis.'

Camilla weighed the satchel and made a little face. 'Not heavy at all.'

'Dynamite. Handle with care.'

'This absolutely isn't you. Whatever you think you feel about her.'

Charlie closed Camilla's hand around the handles of the satchel. 'Put it somewhere inconspicuously safe, and if anything happens to me –'

'Oh do stop. Because I heard you; Fred Kirby.'

The telephone was ringing.

'Forgive me.'

Camilla leaned and kisses him on the cheek. 'You always were my favourite idiot.'

Charlie was saying, 'Yes, yes. Of course. In which case I'll wait. Happily.'

60

13. *Crucifixion.* A hotel bedroom, its shutters open on to a Riviera with a sandy beach, sailing boats, a palm tree. The TV, at an acute angle to the frame, depicts the same scene. Acrylic on paper. 40 x 32.

61

The big room at Mitcheldene & Cleverley occupied most of the first floor. Marcus Steele stood at the wired lectern with his back to tall, wide windows overlooking Manchester Square. In front of him, dealers and *flâneurs* sat at a three-sided square of baize-topped tables. Rows of tight chairs, for tourists, were ranged behind almost as far as the double glass doors, with brass handles, at the back of the room, where three or four old hands liked to stand. As Charlie came in, a grey-bearded porter, in a green baize apron and bib, was parading the next lot.

'Lot 23. Two sixteenth-century carved cherry-wood figures, in the grotesque style, originally from Westphalia. A hundred pounds for them?'

Charlie took a catalogue from the stack on the table by the double doors, glanced at the reticent W.S. Pond clock on the wall to the right and spread himself on two of the row of vacant chairs at the back of the room. He put his padded jacket on the back of one but kept his long fawn scarf coiled loosely around his neck and down into his lap.

Marcus was saying, 'One fifty. Two hundred at the back of the room. At two hundred. Two twenty? At two hundred and twenty then. Two fifty? Any more anywhere? All done? At two hundred and fifty pounds then. Konradi.'

When the door opened behind Charlie, he did not look round. A dealer in a camel-hair coat and silk scarf glanced at him as if he might be an *objet de valeur*, then recognized him possibly, hesitated and, observing no responsive symptom in Charlie's eyes or posture, walked on. Charlie lifted one leg across the other, put one hand on his raised ankle and considered his dated shoes. As the auction proceeded, he took an apparent interest, punctuated by glances at the clock, in various items and people in the room.

'Lot 115,' Marcus said. 'Hand-made Georgian travelling case, said – on good authority – to be by Francesco Pasquale, once owned by Lord Byron. Particularly comely piece, this. Thank you, Mr Konradi, for agreeing! Two hundred and fifty pounds for it? Three hundred on my right. And four. Four hundred and fifty pounds. At four hundred . . . Five hundred at the back of the room. At five hundred pounds then. Lord Marsden, thank you very much.'

As the room began to empty, Marcus stepped down from the lectern and came to where Charlie was in no hurry to leave. 'I was beginning to wonder why you were here, Charlesworth.'

'I was somewhat wondering the same thing.'

'Mill indicated that you were still – what? – in the lists.'

Charlie said, 'I'm not the person you supposed.' He pulled open the right-hand door, relooped his scarf around his neck and went into the small gallery where items from forthcoming sales were encased. 'Possibly not even the one I supposed.'

Pierre-Henri Drot was inspecting some early Persian bronze figurines, one a miniature bell, a tiny ball in an oval cage. He was diplomatically unsurprised to see Charlie. As they shook hands, Pierre-Henri was already leaning towards Marcus. They embraced, chest to chest, looking over each other's shoulders, as Charlie went on down the wide stairs to the ground floor.

He stood on the kerb, the Wallace Collection to his left, and rewound his scarf. A woman went by on an unpainted bicycle. Then a taxi came in from the direction of Wigmore Street. The door opened, a few yards from where Charlie was waiting, and no one got out. Charlie walked a step or two and looked in.

Katya Lowell was sitting in the further corner. It was as if she had contrived a personal shadow around herself. A copious black silk coat fell in two panels over her knees. The surface of the material appeared to be glazed with dark green.

'You waited,' she said.

'I said I would.' He leaned into the cab, as if to be sure that no one else was there.

Her face, in shadow, was unusually pale. 'I'm sorry.'

'Never be that.' He got into the cab. The driver sat looking ahead. He might have been primed to be patient. As Charlie bent forward to give the driver the address, he could see, reflected in the glass, that Katya was turning to look through the back window. When he settled back beside her, he allowed a little distance between them.

'All right?'

Katya said, 'All right?'

'He didn't want you to come. But you did. Thank you.'

'He told me to tell you something.'

'Did he so? And what was that?'

'That his door was always open.'

'Is that as nice of him as it sounds?'

'Does it sound nice?'

'I don't think so.'

'He's changed. Not much. But with Jarvis not much can be . . . more than one thinks.'

'You're afraid.'

'Yes, I am. For you.'

'I shall never let you go, Katya Lowell. No matter what.'

'That's what I'm afraid of.'

'That makes me happier than you may well imagine.'

'Something else I was afraid of.'

The traffic was slow down Park Lane. Charlie had time to look at her.

'It makes you beautiful. Fear. You know that. Perhaps that's why you can't bring yourself to let go.'

'I'm not worth it, Charlie. He showed you, didn't he? What we do when I'm there?'

Charlie said, 'Some of it. But it makes no difference. It makes no bloody difference whatever. A man who does that, he's beaten already. Who does that and does other things. That man knows that he can't ever . . .'

'. . . Allow you to threaten him.'

'The threat doesn't come from me. It comes from what he knows of himself. That's why we – you – can be free of him.'

'Perhaps if I were, I'd no longer be . . . what I want to be. Remember the wound and the bow.'

'Bugger the wound and the bow.' Charlie turned and put his arms around her, the left between the panels of the silk coat, and pulled her to him and kissed her pale mouth and she cried out, 'Ah!'

He withdrew his left hand and looked at the fingers.

'Now you know what you're up against.' She twisted, with care, and looked out of the back window.

'What're you afraid of? There's no one there.'

'That's what,' she said. 'I'm afraid of. He doesn't need to find out what he knows already. Where you live, for instance. That's how he . . . likes to do things.'

The cab went to South Kensington, along the Old Brompton Road, and turned off at Onslow Gardens.

Katya said, 'Where are we going?'

'Boating against the current,' he said. He helped her out of the cab and gave money to the driver with his right hand. 'Stay here for eight or nine minutes, would you, please? If we don't come back, well, that should take care of it.'

Theo Plant opened the front door and was not surprised to see them. He made no remark as Charlie led Katya Lowell to a chair in the hall and had her sit down.

'What did he do to you? Let me see.'

She said, 'It's nothing. Why are we here?'

'Because it's not a number anyone is likely to think of. I want to see what he did.'

'He didn't. He has people who do things. When I ask them, usually.'

'Only this wasn't usual. Am I right?'

'I've never seen him lose control like that before. That was what was different.'

'He knows he's lost you. Will lose you. Anyone who loses control has lost everything. He's afraid you know that.'

'No, no, that's not the kind of fear that'll make him back away. He's more dangerous now than before. He told me to tell you, the blood . . . wasn't for him, or me; it's for you.'

'These men. Was Cater one of them?'

'Cater, no. Cater only comes and goes.'

'Reg. I'm sure he was.'

'They don't have names. They have things they do.'

'I'm going to take you abroad. Somewhere . . .'

'There's no such place.'

'Your new coat, when did you get it? It does matter. To me. Today? Before or after? I don't know which is worse.'

'Worse for whom?'

'You're right: it wouldn't have made any difference to you if he hadn't given it to you at all. But that's not what he thought. And that's why you're smiling. For a second. That's part of what you like about . . . what happens when you're with him.'

'Of course.'

'But not the only part. Because if it were, then you wouldn't . . .'

'. . . Like it. No. I'm sorry, but you're right.'

'Harry Groves.'

She said, 'That was nothing to do with Jarvis.'

'How can you know that? What was Harry Groves to you?'

'A man. Quite a dangerous man.'

'To you?'

'I didn't matter to Harry, one way or the other.'

'You went to Royalton House to see him, didn't you? Why?'

'Because . . . it pleased me to do so.'

'What did he do that . . . pleased you?'

'I'm going to disgust you, is that what you're hoping? Give you a reason to think I'm . . . what I really am maybe. And then . . .'

'You can't. Disgust me. That's the reason I'm asking. So that you can know that.'

'I went there . . .'

'Because Jarvis wanted you to. Why? Did Groves do the same kind of things to you that Jarvis does? Did?'

'No. Not to me.'

'Meaning?'

'You know what.'

'Other women.'

'Nothing queer about Harry Groves.'

'And then . . . you stopped going there, is that right?'

'Yes.'

'Because . . .' Charlie looked at her. There was a little more colour in her cheeks. He looked at his fingers, the blood. 'He didn't need you to. He thought something might happen to you, Jarvis.'

'Not at all.'

Charlie looked at her and she at him and she nodded just a fraction, knowing that he had guessed. 'You told Jarvis that you didn't need to go to Royalton House any more. That you were . . . ready. Why?'

'Because I was.'

'So that night, when you came here with him, this house, with Groves, that was . . . towards the end of your . . . having anything to do with him.'

'To tell you the truth, I never saw him again after that night.'

'When you . . . did what, after you left here?'

'Jarvis wanted me to see Harry because he wanted to know what a brave man looked like when he knew he'd come to the end of the road. Harry knew how to look death in the face.'

'I see. Do I? I think I do. You . . . did a what . . . a portrait? A drawing.'

'He sat for me. He enjoyed it.'

'And when he was dead, did you do one then?'

'No. I had no idea what was . . . going to happen to him.'

'Do you wish you had?'

'He was brave. I like bravery. Despite what he did sometimes.'

'Is Jarvis brave, do you think?'

'Cunning people think there always has to be something cleverer than being brave.'

'And are they right?'

'Depends how clever they are.'

'No one is ever going to hurt you again.'

Katya Lowell said, 'I do rather fear that you're the nicest man in the whole world.'

'Rather uncalled for, that, isn't it?'

She said, 'Does it still stand, Charlie?'

'Does what? Yes. Of course it does.'

She said, 'I hate to say this, but I . . . I should like to marry you very much indeed.'

He looked at her and then he said, 'I understand.'

He led her upstairs and through the vacant domed room and opened the door at the back on to the iron steps which took them on to the terrace and along to where they could go down to the little gate on to the side of Onslow Gardens.

62

21. *The Night Watch.* An avenue of chestnut trees in heavy bud in spring sunshine. Wild flowers in the meadow beyond. To the left of the flowers, a snared rabbit is chewing its trapped leg. A small girl is watching, holding some lettuce leaves, one between her lips. Oil on canvas. 40 x 28.

63

'It's not exactly out of the way,' Charlie said, 'but I thought you might like it. No one else knows the address. I don't know if you care all that much about the light, but they promise me it's very good for . . . what you do.'

'How long have you had this place?'

'A few months now.'

'Have you given up Beaufort Street?'

'Not at all. Truth to tell, this is the first time I've been up here since they first showed it to me.'

'Who did . . . all this?' She had taken one step up the new pine staircase that led up to the wide platform where there was a big bed and new built-in cupboards. 'It's very . . . tactful.'

'Michael Carlotti. Friend of Marcus Steele's.' Charlie went to a painted tallboy with many small drawers in it. He opened the second drawer down on the left-hand side and took out a jeweller's box. Katya was standing in the wide rectangle of brightness that fell from the sloping skylight above them. He held the box out to her. 'I had it made specially for today. Whenever that might be.'

She said, 'Charlie, one thing . . .'

'No, no.' He walked to the back of the studio and behind the wide work surface to the refrigerator. 'Simply . . . ask me for everything and then discard whatever you don't want.'

She was holding his ring to the light. She did not

put it on until he had come back with a bottle of Louis Roederer *brut* and two stemmed glasses.

'I told them to keep it simple. It only has to last for ever.'

He took the ring and slid it on to her finger. The steel shackle was still there, next to it.

Katya said, 'Charlie . . .'

'I know,' he said, 'I know. And of course. Of course not.'

'But I have to say it. Whatever you do, whatever happens . . .'

'I'm well aware.'

'Never imagine me . . .'

'I have no need to. I accept you totally, Katya Lowell. Without quibble or illusion. Now it's lunchtime. Without frivolity, too. Never imagine that. Styles are not men. Motives are not reasons, nor reasons motives. I've been a bit of a fool at times, but I'm quite tired of it. I want you to, no, not be happy, even if I should indeed be glad if you were. I want you to be . . . *unshadowed*. What do you say to next Wednesday?'

'For what?'

'Getting married. One has to give notice, I believe. You haven't been married before or anything complicating like that, have you?'

She said, 'Make no mistake . . .' She caught a tear on the flat of her first finger. 'This is the best day of my life.'

'*A* best day. We must hope to do better.'

'Oh, Charlie!'

'Shall I make the arrangements?'

'You seem to be very good at it.'

'Is there anyone you want to be there at all?'

'Be a good idea if you were. No, I have no family.'

'My sister Camilla and her husband, is it all right if they . . . ?'

'Of course. Charlie, I have to go.'

He said, 'Can I take you somewhere? Where is it you want to go?'

'I never said I wanted to. I said I had to. Please don't say anything.'

64

'Juicy, old boy,' Fred Kirby said. 'Between juicy and extra juicy. We must be very close to "Snip, snip and Bob's your Auntie" time.'

'Don't let's pull the trigger yet, Frederick. More to come, possibly. I just wanted to put down a marker. It's not inconceivable that something might happen to me. Not likely, but . . . not inconceivable.'

'Suits me, old son. Your scoop, your trigger. Trust Fred. Millions do; but you can. Meanwhile, with your permission, the *Crusader* can raise one or two mild worries about whether Green, Wilment is liable for a . . . correction in the short to medium term. All right?'

'Your call', Charlie said, 'in that department.'

'Our friend is up to number twenty-three, if that does anything to whet your appetite.'

'Twenty-three what?'

'In the list of the richest men in England. Tasty prospect, taking him off at the ankles. Always assuming my proprietor wouldn't prefer him on a pedestal. We lives and we learns, do we not, Master M, some of us, occasionally?'

Charlie walked from Fred Kirby's Cheapside office to the tube station at Mansion House. He stood at the top of the steps for a moment and then walked on, down Queen Victoria Street and then down to the Embankment. He walked as if he were with a companion who would not let him go. He walked on again, all the way to the Houses of Parliament. He did not go down the steps to the tube station, but he paused for a moment, as if to say goodbye to someone who, after all, disposed him to walk on. In the end, he walked all the way back to Beaufort Street. He was unlocking the front door when the street lights came on.

There were several large cardboard boxes on the floor of the flat. He removed books and, after inspection, dropped them into the appropriate box under the unreliable shelf. He neither sighed nor smiled. Now and again he read a page or two.

When the telephone rang, he had a book in his hand. He put it back on the shelf and went to the alcove where the drop-leaf stood.

'Hullo.'

A man's voice said, 'Lord Marsden? Katya Lowell.' It was the statement of a topic.

'Who's speaking?'

'That is Lord Marsden, isn't it?'

'That is.'

'Have you got transport?'

'Who is this?'

'Go to 71 Sutherland Villas, SE3. If you want to.'

'And why would I want to?'

Sutherland Villas was a row of two-storey yellow-brick artisans' dwellings. Clipped privet hedges showed above the low walls confronting the slope of the pavement. Tall orange street lamps shed charmless light on repainted front doors and glared on the roofs of the ordinary cars parked on both sides of the hill.

Charlie paid the taxi-driver and stood in the street. A bulb shone, behind net curtains, in the upstairs window of number 71. He opened the wooden gate and took the two paces needed to reach the front door. A splinter of light lay across the top step. He could push the door open. As he did so, he heard the sound of a car starting somewhere down to his left. He turned and watched the green Mercedes go up and then turn right along a better-lit road.

The downstairs room might have been a repository for items destined for a charity sale. A two-wheeled florist's barrow rested on wooden stumps. There were tin flower pots on its three shelves. Some contained sad tulips. Leaning in the corner of the room was a triple mirror. Its chain drooped over the tilted glass. In front of it Charlie could see a blue china saucer, some bottles, an antique telescope and a fencing mask. An open-fronted doll's house had a toy car parked in its garage. Charlie stayed there for a few minutes, as he might at a distasteful art exhibition, and then he went into the narrow yellow hallway and looked up the wooden stairs. They creaked as he climbed them. It was a small house. Three doors led off the landing. One was open. He waited for a moment and he heard a voice say, 'Get her clothes off.'

Charlie took a deep breath and walked into the room from which the voice had come. It was empty. A tape-recorder was running on an unfolded card-table of the kind used in suburban whist drives. There were stains and burns on the torn baize.

The recorded voice said, 'When I tell you to. And shut the window.' Charlie heard the scrape and thump of a window being closed. He was looking at the floor between the table and the wall to his left. It was covered with a litter of Polaroid photographs. They proved to be more deliberately arranged than was at first obvious.

A female voice said, 'Please.'

'That is your wish.'

'Yes.'

Charlie listened to the rest of it as if he were enduring a punishment that was also a terrible pleasure. When the tape clicked off, Charlie nodded twice, a man who had taken the point, and looked more closely at the parade of Polaroids. He again nodded, duly informed, and walked on to the landing. He hesitated for a moment, as if awaiting further instruction. He looked at the closed doors and then he went down the stairs. He stopped under the hall light, in its blue shade. There was a creak on the stair. He looked up and she was coming down, in that fine long coat and black boots.

'So now you know,' she said.

'I know only that I love you. Everything else is . . . décor!'

She stopped on the second stair from the bottom and then she came down quickly and into his arms.

65

The Gritti's *motoscafo* took them from the airport across the lagoon and up to the hotel's wooden landing stage at the mouth of the Grand Canal. Katya was wearing a new top coat, thick grey wool encircled, four times, and then around the collar, with bands of fine silver fox fur. There was a matching hat. She had worn it to the ceremony at Chelsea Town Hall. Charlie chose to admire it, even though (and Camilla guessed) it was as if Jarvis Green was giving away the bride. Charlie was wearing a Burberry with a blue and green plaid lining and a useful hat.

Katya had never before been to Venice. They walked to San Marco and considered the stolen horses and then they went along the Piazzetta and watched Adam and Eve being expelled on the corner of the Doge's palace and decided against having dinner at Harry's Bar. They went back to the hotel and sat on the terrace of their suite and drank *prosecco* and watched the traffic on the canal. Charlie had supper sent up. As they were spooning *zabaglione,* Katya said, 'Charlie . . .' and he said, 'There's no need. I told you. My love for you is . . . unconditional.'

The next morning they went the slow way, by gondola, to Murano and watched red-hot glass being blown into an incandescent globe. She held his arm as the soft bulb was rolled in pigment. She was warm with pleasure at the process. Afterwards, as they sat on the quay and drank their *capucc'*, she closed the fur around her throat. They enjoyed the brisk agility of the conductor as he roped the next *vaporetto* to the railing of the stop and, it seemed, undid it almost all in one prolonged gesture.

Katya said, 'I always hoped that I would meet someone who deserved my love and to whom I'd want to give it with all my heart, and I always feared . . .'

'Having nothing to fear. You don't.'

'. . . That it would come too late.'

Charlie watched another *vaporetto* sidle to the landing stage. 'Consider the possibility that it was . . . too early.'

He agreed with the smile that she gave him. 'Oh, Charlie, I do love you.'

'At my prep school', he said, 'they used to call crying "lobbing". Rhyming slang for "sobbing", possibly. But not the same thing. At all. Lunchtime possibly?'

The *vaporetto* took them past the Palazzo Mocenigo to the Rialto. They walked along a dark trench of tall masonry a few yards down from the Rialto bridge to the Trattoria alla Madonna. Then they walked to the Scuola San Rocco where Charlie sat on a polished bench trying to admire the translation of the Duino Elegies that Katya had given him. She lay on the floor – he loved that – and studied the figures swimming on Tintoretto's ceiling through a little brass telescope. He was careful not to be looking when she turned it on him.

They ate a long dinner at Anice Stellata and talked

of going to Trieste the next time they came to Italy. 'No art to worry about,' Katya said. 'Perhaps that's what Rilke liked about the place. Nothing to make him feel small.'

'No amount of art will ever worry me,' Charlie said. 'I can look at you while you look at it and you can put its lights out.'

They ambled along the Riva degli Schiavoni and drank coffee at the Caffè Quadri. People looked at Katya, but no one approached them. He told her how, when Bismarck was dumped by the Kaiser and granted a princedom as a sop, he remarked that he would use the title when he wanted to travel incognito. 'Lady Marsden can serve in the same office, if you want it to. What's important is that you remain Katya Lowell, the painter.'

'I will,' she said. 'The boys're stacking the chairs. They want to go to bed. Or something. So do I.'

As they were watching the lights floating across the ceiling of the quiet bedroom, she said, 'That was perfect.'

'Anywhere you want to go,' he said, 'or live, is where we'll go and where we live.'

'Never doubt that I love you, Charlie, will you?'

'You doubt love's range,' he said. 'I don't.'

'With all my heart,' she said.

'But that's as far as it goes?'

'You promised to be patient. I couldn't be happier than I am with you.'

'Did I hear you close your eyes by any chance?'

'No, but I did.'

After breakfast they walked to the Doge's Palace.

Charlie said, 'The one Doge I never fail to think of is Marino Falieri. The one they thought they could efface for ever.'

'What can't be done is always what people want to do.'

'He's a snake,' Charlie said. 'I want to kill him.'

'Kill him, you kill us.'

'If you knew . . .'

'I do know. That's why . . . you must never do anything . . .'

'You grant him too much. All he is is a peculating clerk, on a grand scale. Fred Kirby has all the facts. Nothing can happen to me, and Jarvis knows it, without his castle falling down.'

'I know that.'

His silence said that he had noticed how quickly she had said it. He had dropped behind her as they went into the Doge's courtyard and headed for the steps. She seemed to have been left alone. She turned her head and said, 'It's not true.' She looked for him left and right and then there he was. 'I swear to you.'

'What isn't?'

'I married you because I love you and because you love me and your love is the most important thing in the world to me.'

'Is what isn't true?' He was gallant enough to smile.

'You mustn't joke.'

'*Ever*?'

'What isn't true is what you didn't say but I . . .

suspected you were thinking. What does "peculating" mean?'

'It means he's a fraudster, a sneak thief raised to the nth degree.'

'He didn't mind me seeing you, at first. Because that . . .'

'Put salt on it.'

'But then he . . . tried to stop me. You must realize that. That's why he . . . hurt me . . . had me hurt, the way you . . .'

'. . . Were meant to discover. I'm well aware. It's not even worth talking about.'

'I married you because I loved you and because . . . I need your love. Don't spoil it by making a . . . vocation of hating Jarvis. It promotes him above his station. Love me and . . . nothing else. Trust me, Charlie, please.'

'*And* love you?' he said.

The trace of sadness that crossed her face pleased him more than he would have wished.

66

26. *Do We Not Bleed?* A heavy tenement in the Venice ghetto with a kosher dairy on the ground floor with broken windows. Pencil on hotel stationery. 22 x 16.

67

The Gritti's *motoscafo* took them to the airport on a grey morning. As they drove, with rich bumps, away from the city and along the alley between the black, toothy piles, the waters of the lagoon lost their reflected glory. Charlie and Katya sat on the cushioned benches in the stern. 'That was . . . everything I hoped,' she said.

'Might I be a little sorry to know that?'

'Please don't be. I mean it.'

He had the fur hem of her sumptuous coat between his fingers. His silence was more articulate that she cared to know. She pulled away gently, leaning to her left. She looked at his smile and saw the pain. She stood up on the buff-coloured cushioned seat in the stern and allowed the wind to make wings of the unbelted coat. She inclined her body towards Charlie, and it was enough to let the wind take the coat under her shoulders and then drive it down her outstretched arms. Charlie raised a hand, but she denied him and allowed the coat to fly free and flap, like a sudden rare and clumsy bird, bound for the distant cemetery island. Then it dipped, caught water, went lame and dropped into the heavy waves.

'I mean it, Charlie. I'd sooner die than . . . have you doubt me.'

Charlie said, 'I understand.'

'What?'

'I'll have Fred burn what I gave him. All of it.'

'No need,' she said. 'As long as . . . you never ask me . . .'

'It shall never be mentioned again. Unless it's by you.'

She came and sat close to him. His arm, and part of the Burberry, embraced her. 'And until then you'll . . . despise me,' she said.

'Never.'

She took his hand and counted the fingers, and then she dared to look at him.

Charlie said, 'That's why I shall never quite be able to take his place, isn't it?'

68

12. *Hurry While Stocks Last.* A medieval village with a store selling the wooden benches and foot-stalls in which convicted persons were penned and humiliated. Pen and ink. Original of a cartoon for *Foolscap*, a defunct literary quarterly. 18 x 12.

69

Charlie disposed of the lease for the flat in Beaufort Street. He and Katya went to live in Tite Street. Her work did not change greatly, but there was the odd levity for Charlie to smile at. He took it as a sign of generosity; but he was not fooled. They were happy together, but she was not as happy as she might be; if happiness was what was lacking. He did not stay in the studio when she was working. He made no virtue of his tact, but he did contrive to be absent for long periods of the day.

The sale of the Irish house was made, rather more richly than he had expected, to a syndicate that proposed to turn the mansion into a clubhouse for a new golf course. Camilla was eager to have Marsden Old Place renovated so that Piers and Caroline could enjoy the same sort of childhood days that she and Charlie remembered before their mother died.

Charlie admired whatever work Katya had done, when she invited inspection, but he assumed no proprietary stance. Her work was hers, never his; so, although he never said as much, was her time. He felt no conscious relief, or feeling of any kind, that he received no word, no indication of menace, from Jarvis Green. Fred Kirby called him a couple of times but was, it seemed, content to wait on springing the trap under Jarvis.

Charlie loved Katya's generosity. She honoured his love with all the charm and, when needed, the elegance he had admired from the first. She made love with every sign of pleasure. They went to the theatre rarely and to concerts more often. They were there to applaud the first night of *Whodunnit*. Katya was photographed as if she were the star of the movie. Benedict Bligh said, 'Hullo.'

When Rollo Farber came to the studio he saw happy signs of a new Katya, less strict, freer in the use of paint. 'You've obviously made her happy, you lucky sod.'

Charlie was not deceived; nor did Katya make any show of deceiving him. Charlie knew, night after night, that he had pleased her up to a certain point. He could do no more.

One morning, quite some time after they had started living together in Tite Street, he said, 'I'm off to have a swim and then, later, if it's all right with you, I'm thinking of buzzing down to Marsden Old Place with Timmy Lethers and seeing what can be done about restoring the blue drawing-room. Quite a full day it promises to be. Be back this evening, though. Don't fancy a break possibly, do you?'

She said, 'I really ought to work.'

'It's coming along incredibly well, as you do not need me to say.'

'I'll probably . . . go out later.'

He said, 'You do know one thing above all, don't you?'

'Yes.'

'You must do what you want. Because it's what I want, for you.'

'No one shall ever know, Charlie. No one. Never from me. And not from anyone else.'

'People always do know eventually, my darling, though it rarely takes that long. Think of B.B. It's of no consequence to me. I told you that my love was eternal and that's . . . what it is and will be. Despite appearances and incidentals, I have it on excellent authority that you and I will always be . . . what we are.'

She held him for a moment, close. 'Will you come and get me later?'

'Elgin Avenue?'

'Why not? Eight-thirty.'

'I'll be there. Number 38, shall we say? I shall have a book. I always do these days. Never fear. If you're later, you're later. We can eat or not, as you wish.'

'Why are you so nice to me?'

'In the hope that it's one of the things you want.'

He drove Tim Lethbridge down to Marsden Old Place in the renovated Morgan for which he had swapped the Alvis and some change. Tom Cheale had arranged for a local builder, whose father had worked for the old Viscount, to come to the house, along with Sam Randall, a carpenter who specialized in restoring old woodwork. Charlie was pleased to behave as they would wish, at once informal and in the expectation that they were men who valued the antique standards of their crafts. Tim Lethbridge noticed certain variations in the pitch and pacing of Charlie's speech. Neither patronizing nor matey, he presumed that men of quality would do nothing less than their best. His manner and stance said what did not need saying.

70

'Please.'

24. *Beware of the Doge.* A gloss on the painting of Marino Falieri, the disgraced fifty-fifth doge of Venice, draped with black (as it is in the Doge's Palace in Venice) but with one corner revealed, displaying a hand with a dull steel ring on one female finger. Oil on board. 28 x 26.

Charlie deposited Tim Lethbridge in Palace Gardens, where he had a flat in a modern block. Charlie happened to know that it had been bequeathed to Tim by his late lover, who had had an antique shop in South Moulton Street. There was an unspoken fidelity in Lethers's decision not to sell the place, even though it was not to his taste.

Charlie had allowed plenty of time to drive across the park. The lacklustre pomposity of the buildings in the elongated curve of Elgin Avenue promised that it was not the sort of street in which he was likely to see anyone he knew. Owing to the wide presence of a removals van, he had to double-park the Morgan in order to honour being where he said he would be, outside number 38, which otherwise had no significance. He looked at his watch only to be sure that he was not late. He was early. He opened his window slightly, and then he went on rereading *Decline and Fall*. Drizzle spotted the narrow windscreen.

It was ten to nine, pretty much the hour he had expected, when a new green Mercedes grew fatter in Charlie's mirror. It stopped short of where the Morgan was parked. He put a mark in his book and slotted it behind his seat. Katya was wearing a slim dark-leather coat and black boots. She put out a hand to the drizzle and then walked quite quickly to where Charlie was waiting. He leaned across and opened the door by the pantechnicon.

'Have I kept you waiting a very long time?'

'I only just got here,' Charlie said. 'Lucky I didn't keep you waiting.'

'You are good,' she said.

'Can't be helped now,' he said.

She leaned and kissed him and took his hand.

Charlie said, 'Only one thing stands between us and . . . perfect happiness, doesn't it?' She smiled again and so did he. 'The very slight suspicion that it's not entirely what . . . either of us want. And we also know why.'

'You've never called me by my name,' she said.

'Katya?' he said. 'Have I not? Surely . . .'

'I've saved it', she said, 'for someone I can trust. Karen.'

'Karen it is then. Karen.'